PULSE
RESPONSE

PULSE
RESPONSE

JEFF BEASLEY

PULSE RESPONSE

iUniverse books may be ordered through booksellers or by contacting:

iUniverse
1663 Liberty Drive
Bloomington, IN 47403
www.iuniverse.com
844-349-9409

ISBN: 978-1-6632-4219-8 (sc)
ISBN: 978-1-6632-4214-3 (e)

Print information available on the last page.

iUniverse rev. date: 07/11/2022

To my family, Kim, Damon/Heather, Dana/Sam

Thanks to my friends,

Willie, Ed, Krist, Bill, and Rolfe

Thanks to Joe Bullock, author of "Walking With Herb" for your advice and guidance.

I just stepped out of the doors to the university's engineering and science library. I had just submitted my Ph.D. dissertation after having obtained all of the appropriate signatures and university approvals, answered all of the graduate editor's comments and obtained my advisor's and committee's blessing. It was quite a remarkable feeling walking out the doors of the library knowing that I had completed something very few people will ever experience. But it was also a rather empty moment because when I walked out the door, no one was there, only a few students were walking by, but definitely no cheering crowd was waiting to congratulate me, the newest member of the academic community, Dr. Josh Baker!

But I couldn't let the moment go without some celebration, so I yelled out, saying, "You did it dude" and gave myself a high five and saying, "Way to go Dr. B". I think some of the people walking by thought I was crazy and maybe I was a little bit, working on the doctorate in Electrical Engineering is a lot of work. The truth is it probably did make me a little crazy. Too many late nights working on my research, too many last-minute demands by my advisor and let us not forget class homework/exams, qualifying exams, comprehensive exams, and all the requisite presentations, and peer reviewed publications required to justify my contribution to the 'body of knowledge'.

"So, what's next," I said to myself. Well, I've got a job waiting for me, it's actually on the same university campus where I earned my doctorate, it is with the university's prestigious engineering research lab (ESL). In fact, the job is with the cyber security group whose members included scientists and engineers from the NSA, FBI, CIA, Department of Defense and Homeland Security and various private contractors. It's a pretty cool job that allows me to continue work in my research area. My research had been critically reviewed and accepted by scientists from the national labs, industry, and the military which is why I think I landed the job with ESL.

My research work is actually with testing integrated circuits not cyber security so why am I going to work with a cyber-security group? I guess they will explain this to me tomorrow when I start to work. During the course of my research, I did figure out a way to determine if a device is defective by simply analyzing the transient currents generated when the device power ups, called pulse response testing. Actually, it wasn't that simple. There are a lot of things that have to be done correctly to generate valid and consistent results. To me this was pretty exciting because I was able to extract subtle features from the complex current waveforms just by looking at how the device powered up and running some complex computer algorithm to make a pass/fail decision. I determined that a change in the waveform indicated the device has some type of defect and should be classified as a fail. I told the military guys, when they were reviewing my research, that wouldn't they prefer to have integrated circuits in their weapons and vehicles that were known to be defect free and did not have a potential to fail. They weren't impressed. They said I would never be able to extract any useful information from the extremely noisy transient current waveform especially with the expected increase in transistor count.

I also presented my work to representatives from the automotive industry since electronics has become a major contributor to all aspects of modern automobiles, which includes ignition control, braking, improving gas mileage, safety improvements and controlling everything else inside your car. Wouldn't they like a sensor that would tell you how your car is feeling? I know that cars tell you when it needs to go see a tech for service with the blinking "service needed" light but wouldn't it be cool to know how your car is feeling today, not just when something has failed. I told the "reps" from the automotive industry that we could do this. Your car would actually be able to tell you how it is feeling. In fact, it could say, "I felt better yesterday. I think something is getting ready to fail." I know this is pretty weird and unfortunately the "auto" guys felt the same. I never did any follow-up work with them.

A by-product of my research showed that I could also detect changes in the power-up waveform due to the fact that the devices were made at a different fabrication run or by a different manufacturer. The same part generated a different waveform hence, possibly the reason I was joining the cyber security team at ESL. They said that their goal is to use my techniques to see if we can detect devices whose internal architecture could have possibly been altered. Altered devices could potentially create a threat to our cyber infrastructure and national security. It is not too far-fetched of an idea to realize that integrated circuits that are made globally could easily have the chips architecture altered, even with all the security that the manufacturers have in place. The altered chips would still provide the same intended functionally but might also include a backdoor, or a way to eavesdrop or alter data streams or even trigger an event all for malicious purposes. Can you imagine the consequences of having a microprocessor configured to broadcast an encrypted wireless message containing the access codes for our military's arsenal or that a military weapon was actually being controlled remotely? And let's not forget about the safety of our power-grid and protecting it from outside threats. It is a little overwhelming to think about this.

Walking down the International Mall outside the library I smiled to myself. I thought I had it made. Everything was in place, a great degree, a cool place to work, and my wife, a beautiful French woman and two remarkable kids. I had told my wife that this research was going to change our lives but if I had only known what was waiting for us.

2

I was quite surprised when I passed through the security gates at ESL. There were signs everywhere saying, "Welcome Dr. Baker!!" This was quite a welcome surprise, I don't think my Ph.D. advisor ever once said thank you or anything else to me, it was always, "did you get the paper done?" It was really just about him. Of course, I was just one of his students and that was my job, to make him look good and I did make him look good. I think this is true for almost all Ph.D. students. Sadly, it's an unfortunate rite of passage when pursuing an advanced degree

"Hey Dr. Baker!" said a staff member who greets me at the security gates. "I am here to take you to your office." We walked down the hall and climbed the stairs to the second floor. The office was at the end of the hall and I was surprised to find a nicely laid out office that even has a window. The room was quite roomy compared to the cramped graduate office I used for three years. I felt I was definitely ready to take on the world.

I began to unpack my backpack and set up my office. Yes, I am still carrying a backpack, the same one I carried throughout graduate school. It has been good luck for me so why change now. I set out a picture of my wife, Adeline, I call her Ade (pronounced Adie), our two kids, Sara and Sean, and our two dogs, Moco and Tobi. A real nuclear family. Sara and Sean are the joys of our lives, and they keep us focused on what is important. We are lucky parents. Moco is a German Shepherd and probably smarter than most people.

Sometimes this can be a challenge. But I have to admit that while working on my dissertation I did have many conversations with Moco, in fact, I think Moco might have suggested, or maybe sniffed out some solutions for extracting unique features that will help identify defective devices. Of course, Mocos's favorite solution was a dog treat and playing with the ball. At that she excelled.

Tobi is part Doberman and just full of love. I think that is her way of getting the upper hand on people. She knows she is a tough breed of dog, but let the people think there is no threat, get them close and then she attacks. Actually, she doesn't attack, she just growls, shows her teeth and then rolls over and says pat my tummy. She's a good guard dog.

I continued unpacking my backpack and put out a Courting candle. This type of candle sits on top of a wrought iron shaft with a wooden base. Courting candles were used in the old days to limit the amount of time that the bow (boyfriend) could stay while courting his girl. This was a special gift from Ade to remind me that I have to limit my time on my research because I can be obsessive and sometimes don't know when to let things go. She is reminding me that I have kids and a family at home. It's a special reminder for me. Ade is a beautiful but complex woman, not unlike the geodes we have on the mantle of our fireplace. It is also fair to say that she is slightly stubborn and hardheaded. Love you sweetheart. :-) I thought to myself.

Ade found the courting candle at a small antique store when we were traveling through Nashville, Tennessee on our way to the Oak Ridge National Laboratories. I had a research presentation scheduled there. My grandparents are all from Tennessee, so we had a wonderful time visiting my many relatives. Ade really enjoyed looking at the old southern homes, and colonial period antiques. She said that when she retires, she is going to buy and sell antiques. I told her, "That is a good idea since you already have a small museum in our house and a huge inventory in the garage." She just smiled.

I had almost completed unpacking when the same staff member who showed me to my office, walked in the door. "Dr. Baker. I have been asked to let you know that you have a meeting in the conference room in fifteen minutes. The conference room is in room 279, just out the door and to your right. "Oh, my name is Jace, I am one of the engineers assigned to this project. You will meet the rest of the team in the conference room. Welcome to our group." I finished setting up and thought a few minutes about my day so far.

The conference room was quite ornate. A beautifully decorated room and the oak table and chairs made me feel like I was in the presence of royalty, or I was entering a high-level corporate conference room. There were 4 people in the room. As I walked in, the introductions began. My new boss, Dr. Rico, head of the analysis group for ESL introduced me to the group. "Everyone, this is the newest addition to our group, Dr. Josh Baker. Dr. Baker is here to help us with the analysis of the integrated circuits."

"Dr. Baker, this is Dr. Sassenfeld, head of the solid state physics team. His team is investigating the various ways that silicon architecture can be altered undetected." I shook Dr. Sassenfeld's hand and said, "I have heard of the Sassenfeld Criteria in Mathematics, any relation?" Dr. Sassenfeld just smiled.

Dr. Rico introduced the next person, "This is Dr. Krist Hudson. He is with the FBI's cyber security team and is here on special assignment to support our work." I shook Dr. Hudson's hand.

The last person is Annie Pollard, and she is going to serve as your technical assistant. She is also an Electrical Engineer just like you so she should have some idea what you are trying to do, particularly with analysis and testing. I believe you two met while in graduate school. She joined our group after she completed her master's degree. The other person is Jace, who I believe that you have already met.

Dr. Rico and the other people sat down at the custom crafted oak table. "Dr. Baker, as we previously mentioned to you, we have asked you to join our group at ESL for the following reason. Our task is to figure out a way to verify that integrated circuits are doing what they were supposed to do. Industry has many test techniques and test vectors in place to verify functionality of a circuit. Their goals are to provide triple 9's, 99.9% confidence that a device is working properly. The tests are based on standard failure analysis techniques and a set of test vectors that enables the test group at the fab facility to verify the chip is working properly and doing what it is supposed to do. But how do we know that the chip is <u>only</u> doing what it is supposed to do? We are not sure we can fully answer this because a microprocessor chip can perform virtually an unlimited number of tasks. We need a way to detect if a chip has been altered, doing something it is not supposed to do, it's very simple. Dr. Baker, do you think you can do this?"

Dr. Baker looked around at everyone, somewhat perplexed. Everyone looked expectantly at him. This is not a simple task he thought to himself. He had proposed an idea a few years back that bad chips might emit a unique signature or artifact that could be used for classifying the chip to be good or bad. His research did show evidence of this, but he was not able to prove that this unique signature or an artifact existed in all technologies or in chips with different architectures. In fact, the artifact was hidden in different manufacturing runs. Now he was being asked to detect that the chip's internal architecture had been altered. Dr. Baker looks into the expectant eyes around the table and said confidently, "Yes."

"OK", said Dr. Rico, let's get this started. "Annie, you go with Dr. Baker and you two develop an initial testing strategy to get this work started. Dr. Baker, I have arranged for you to receive sample integrated circuits from various silicon foundries around the globe. I already have examples from Taiwan, United States, China, Israel, and South Korea to get us started. I have sent an email to you and Annie that provides the technical data for each chip. Ok, thanks everyone." With that the meeting ended and Dr. Baker thought to himself, "Welcome to the real world."

3

Annie and Dr. Baker walked back to his office. "Dr. Baker", Annie said, "It is an honor to be working with you, I am very familiar with your research, and I think you might have hit on something. It will be fun working with you." Dr. Baker replied, "please call me Josh and thank you for your comments. I wish I was as confident as you."

They arrived back at Josh's office/lab and both immediately began looking at the datasheets for the integrated circuits they would be testing. "Some of these devices are quite complex, this one has over 5 billion transistors," said Annie. "Have you ever tested a device this complex?" "I recently tested an Intel 22-core Xeon processor that had 7.2 billion transistors. We were able to detect the presence of some defects. I believe that we were able to see variations because the device has multiple power supply and ground connections, so it enabled us to monitor multiple points and see above the noise level. There were even power pins for parts of the circuit that required a different voltage and we monitored all of the pins." "Did you monitor all pins separately or did you just combine all currents and analyze the composite waveform?" Asked Annie. "No, we analyzed the transient current generated at each power and ground pin separately. It took a long time to analyze the data but eventually we were able to see subtle differences in the waveforms between different devices. Our results showed us that some of the devices contained different features and it had been verified that these devices were known to contain defects. Our success rate was a little better than a coin toss but not good enough to claim we had perfected the test. The important thing to realize is that not all devices contain this many transistors. This is going to be true for most communication and analog devices that interface to the outside world. This includes devices that are enabled with WiFi and Ethernet connections."

"But we are not trying to detect defects" said Annie "we are trying to detect operational variations that are not consistent with normal device operation. We are supposed to detect that a chip's architecture has been modified. How is analyzing the transient current waveform going to help identify altered chips?"

Josh thought for a moment and said, "The only difference I can think of is that we can expect to see a difference in the transient current signature for the section that has been altered when compared to a <u>known</u> good chip. We just need to know what the transient current for a device that has not been altered looks like. We should be able to obtain sample 'good' chips from the manufacturers." "What if all chips we are examining have been altered?" asked Annie. "For the moment, let's assume that we will have good or unaltered devices. The truth is, we don't currently have a way to even know if any of the devices we received actually have been altered" replied Josh.

They went back to examining the data sheets a little less enthusiastic than they were earlier. This is like a research project, thought Josh. Have I returned to academics? Josh continued reviewing the data sheets while Annie began constructing the test jig for a device from Israel. The next thing Josh realized was it was time to go home. He put his things in the backpack and left the building. The guard at the gate said, "Have a good night Dr. Baker!" Josh thought to himself, "this is a nice place, I think I am going to enjoy this."

Josh arrived at home to cheers of joy from his kids, dogs, and smiling wife. "How was your day" asked Ade. "Definitely interesting. I met a lot of the staff, and they seem like a good group. Remember a few years back that I had a graduate student helping me, her name was Annie? She now works at ESL and has been assigned to work with me. "Hey daddy," asked Josh's youngest. "What's an ESL?" "Hey Big Guy, that is where daddy works now."

4

The next day, Annie began conducting tests on the device from Israel. "Hey Josh, look at the waveform being generated by this device. Does this look normal" asked Annie? Josh carefully studied the waveform. He zoomed in and out and finally said, "It has all of the normal characteristics I would expect to see. Notice the oscillation at the beginning of the transient and how it tails off which is what we expect to see for a power supply transient. It looks similar to transients generated by a logic device. Switch the scope to the FFT mode and let's see if anything interesting is exhibited." Annie changed the settings and immediately a new waveform was displayed. "What we are seeing now is the spectral content of the transient waveform. All these spikes are showing the spectral content of our transient." said Josh. In the early days of our work, we said that you can actually hear if a device is bad by listening to its power-on transient. We demonstrated this to a group of engineers and scientist at the national lab. We looped the recording of the transient waveform and played it for them. You could actually hear the changes in the sound for different chips and different defect types.

"That's pretty bazaar to think that an integrated circuit actually emits a sound." commented Annie. "Yeah, we looked hard for the unique sound that a defect on a chip would make. But once again, we were looking for defects, not devices whose architecture had been altered." said Josh.

There was a knock on the door and Dr. Rico and another gentleman entered. "Dr. Baker, this is Jordan Pines. He is the budget guy for the project. He needs to get some information from you so you can get paid. "Nice to meet you, Jordan," said Josh. "So, I see that you are already getting started with testing the chips. You are taking this seriously," said Jordan. "That is what we are paid to do," said Josh. "We are first looking at a device from Israel." "Have you made any discoveries yet" asked Jordan. "Not yet" said Josh, "we are just getting started." "Do you have any devices from Taiwan, Japan, or France?" asked Jordan. "We have a device from Taiwan, but we haven't tested it yet," said Josh. "We have a new shipment coming in next week and we will have sample chips from Japan, Italy, Costa Rica, France, and India" added Dr. Rico.

"It will be interesting to see what you find," said Jordan. "I just don't see how anyone can actually detect a change in the chip's architecture. Personally, I think it is a waste of time and I am surprised the project was even funded, but that is the government." said Jordan.

Josh was a little surprised by Jordan's comment. "Jordan, I can assure you that we will do an excellent job for ESL and this group. We already have some good ideas ..." "Yea I know, I just think it is a waste of time," said Jordan. "Jordan, you said you had some payroll questions for Dr. Baker", said Dr. Rico. "No, not really, I just wanted to meet the new guy before his project funding gets canceled." Everyone's eyes opened and they all looked at Jordan. "Dr. Baker, I am just joking around, I am sure you are going to do a good job. But I will be checking up on you and your work later on." Dr. Rico stepped in and said, "Dr. Baker, I was wondering if you could join me for lunch today. I know a really good Mexican food place. Do you like green Chile rellenos?" "Sounds good," replied Josh. "My wife and I have always said we stayed in this area for the "Hatch" green Chile. It is somewhat addictive".

With that, the meeting ended, Dr. Rico said "I'll swing by about 11:30 to go to lunch. Does that work for you?" "Sounds good," said

Josh. Dr. Rico and Jordan then left the room. "That was weird," said Annie. "Is that guy actually thinking about pulling the funding for your project? Can he actually do that? We just got started." "I don't know," said Josh. "Jordan is in charge of the budget, and he can make good and bad things happen. I will discuss this with Dr. Rico at lunch."

Annie and Josh continued running various tests on the chip from Israel. Annie said, "right at the moment I don't how we can detect a change in the chips architecture without de-lidding the device and using an electron microscope to examine the chips' layout and then comparing the chip layout to a known good device."

Right at 11:30 Dr. Rico stuck his head in the door and said, "Casi listo? [Almost ready]" Josh smiled and replied, "Si, estoy casi listo, [yes, I am almost ready]." "Dr. Rico, I married a French woman, but she also speaks Spanish," said Josh. "Que bueno" replied Dr. Rico.

They got in the car and the first thing Dr. Rico said was, "Josh, please call me Daniel, Dr. Rico is too formal. Wasn't that meeting with Jordan bazaar. The guy is a pencil pusher and bean counter, and he does oversee the budgets, but he shouldn't be asking you those kinds of questions. He doesn't have the right to be directly involved with our work. And specifically, he is not your boss, that is my job and it is my responsibility to make sure we and you meet the deadlines and satisfy the requirements of the task order." "Thanks Daniel" said Josh. "And besides, that guy is always hiding behind a closed door in his office. We jokingly refer to him as the '*Big Guy*', laughed Daniel. So, we are off to Los Campos Cafe."

The smells of Chile filled the air when we entered Los Campos Café. The restaurant is a quaint old place a few blocks from the old part of historic downtown. This part of town was actually created when the railroad decided to build on the east side of the Rio Grande river. Apparently the price of the land was quite cheaper on this side of the river than on the other side.

Josh ordered the Mexican plate which comes with a chile relleno, tacos, enchiladas and beans. Daniel ordered the relleno plate. "The food is excellent," said Josh. "My wife and I eat here at least once a week," said Daniel. "Josh, thanks for joining me for lunch. I have a few things I wanted to discuss outside of ESL. It really bothered me when Jordan came into your lab this morning and asking all those questions. This project is not top secret, but it does require an L clearance to be able to enter our doors. Jordan's questions about what country the devices you are testing are coming from are not appropriate. I am going to report that to security. I am sure that he is just trying to act like a big shot and pretend that he is part of the team, but we just don't joke around or even openly discuss this. We don't know what we will find when testing these devices from other countries, but we definitely can't be publicly talking about our work".

"So how is it going so far" asked Daniel? "We have been testing the device manufactured in Israel but all we can see are differences between devices that were made during separate fabrication runs. Annie and I have discussed some alternate tests and we also have some new ideas. Jace is going to start running some tests for us this afternoon. I have some ideas about exploring the information we obtain from running a frequency analysis on the pulsed power-on waveform. Jace is going to start collecting information on the power supply rails." "Are you looking at only the V_{DD} pins?" asked Daniel. "No, we have configured the test jig so we can also look at both the ground pins and power supply pins. This test is also not just looking at the current, but it is also looking at the voltage variations." "Do you have any other ideas yet?" asked Daniel. "Yes, we will be de-lidding some of the devices and using a scanning electron microscope to examine the chips layout and then comparing the chip layout to a known good device. At this point, we are just trying everything."

After lunch Josh, Annie and Jace met to discuss their test plans. "Let's go ahead and remove the lids from the devices we have been testing," said Josh. Jace immediately began the de-lidding process. When he was done, he placed the device on the mount for the electron microscope. "It is always fun to look at the chip layout, it looks like we are looking at the roadmap for a city, très magnifique" said Jace. "Yes, it is beautiful, where did you pick up the French?" "I took two years of French in college and spent some time in France as part a foreign exchange program" replied Jace. Josh spoke up and said proudly, "I married a French woman, so I learned the language on the job, also, do you have the image for the device that is known to be good. We need to do an A/B comparison." said Josh. They loaded the known good chip image into the system. They began to do a quick A/B comparison. They didn't find any differences which did not surprise them. "Get Dr. Sassenfeld down here from the Solid State Physics group and let's let him take a look at the images. Maybe he will have another idea for exposing modified devices.

"I just called his office, and he will be down in about 30 minutes" said Annie.

at a semiconductor facility in Corbeil-Essonnes, France .....

I always thought it was funny to run around work wearing a "bunny suit". It makes me feel like I am employed at the Playboy Mansion. The truth is I work on the manufacturing floor for Reese Semiconductor in Corbeil-Essonnes, France. We are in the south suburbs of Paris. I am in charge of the group that oversees the assignment of the photolithography masks used to make integrated circuits. "Etiene, do you have everything uploaded?" asked Pierre. "The fabrication run is beginning". "Yes, all of the masks are in place," smiled Pierre. "We are going to get a nice reward for this work." "How many devices will we have when done?" asked Etiene. "We should have about 2000 finished devices." Said Pierre. At $1,500 each that is a nice chunk of change.

Etiene and Pierre went back to work and the fab run began laying down multiple layers of oxide, polysilicon, metal and doped layers of silicon. The completed chips were next sent to testing and final packaging. Their colleague Philippe, worked in the sorter and packaging group, his job is to sort the fabricated ICs and remove any defective devices and then package the ICs for delivery to the respective customers. Philippe was in the process of packaging the ICs and noticed that a quantity of 30 ICs were to be sent to the United States, a group called ESL [Cyber Security Group] in New Mexico. Phillippe took out his cell phone and called Etiene. "Etiene, we have a potential problem, some of our custom ICs are destined for a research group called the cyber security group in the United States." Etiene replied, "don't worry, we have an inside man with that group, he's got our back."

6

Dr. Sassenfeld, from the Solid State Physics group arrived in Josh's lab and said, "What's up?" We have a device under the electron microscope and we were wondering if you have any suggestions on what we should be looking for?" asked Annie. Dr. Sassenfeld looked at the image on the screen and said "très magnifique". "That's what Jace said" laughed Josh. They immediately began looking at the image that was being displayed by the electron microscope. Dr. Sassenfeld said, "At this time the only thing I can think of doing are A/B comparisons to see if we notice any differences between the two devices. You have to remember that we are only seeing things on the surface of the device, some things could be hidden from us", said Dr. Sassenfeld. "That is where Dr. Baker's work could be most advantageous for us, he is seeing what's happening inside the device. Let me do some more work on this and I'll get back to you guys if I come up with any ideas that can help us identify changes in the architecture of the device. It is possible that we will need to use a Transmission Electron Microscope (TEM) to see under the surface. If Dr. Baker determines that a device has been altered, then maybe we can justify using a TEM. Talk to you guys later"

Annie said, "Dr. Baker, we got a shipment of ICs today from South Korea and France. I will set up a test so we can do pulse response transient analysis testing of the devices. I should have the first group ready to test later this afternoon." "Thanks", replied Dr. Baker.

Annie began testing the devices and asked Dr. Baker, "is this what you were expecting to see in the pulse response?" "Yes, that is the typical response", replied Dr. Baker. "Notice all the weird artifacts at the beginning of the transient. We have examined these artifacts many times in hopes to use this to find or identify that something has changed in the device. In our current project, our goal is to see if we can detect if a device has been altered." "In fact," said Dr. Baker "those weird transients we are seeing are what we used to identify if devices contained a defect. In a way, those artifacts are what are unique to each device, in fact, we can say with some certainty that if the artifacts have changed then the device has changed …" "or been altered" said Annie smiling. "You are exactly correct" said Dr. Baker.

"Did you ever do FFT analysis on the transient?" asked Annie. "Yes, we did" replied Dr. Baker. "In fact, we used the frequencies generated by the FFT to actually listen to see if a device was defective. Our research showed that the bad or defective devices had a unique sound." "Is it possible that altered devices could emit unique sounds?" asked Annie. "Wouldn't it be cool if we could identify altered devices by their unique sound?" said Annie. "I think that's our goal," said Dr. Baker, smiling.

"Annie, let's change our approach and let's focus on seeing if we can identify unique sounds that are being emitted by the devices and to see if we can determine if the sounds being emitted are from a good device or bad or even an altered device." said Dr. Baker. "Sounds good," said Annie. "Let me play around with it a little bit, I have some ideas I learned from my communication classes in grad school that might fit in well with this. Do you remember the mixer circuit Dr. Baker? I think that maybe that could help us shift the frequencies of the artifacts we are seeing in the transients down to audible frequencies. Give me the afternoon to see what I come up with." Annie said, smiling.

Annie used the sample integrated circuits that Dr. Baker brought with him to set up her test circuit to analyze the transient waveform. She used a mixer circuit to shift the frequencies of the transients down to the audible range and began running tests. Surprisingly, she could hear differences in the sounds coming from the each of the devices. What she didn't know yet was what the sounds specifically represent. She wondered, did shifting the transient frequencies have negative effects, specifically was she losing critical information or even unique details that could aid in the detection of defects. Annie continued with the tests, enjoying the sounds that the devices were generating. "I feel like a musical conductor," laughed Annie.

She continued with her work, trying to better refine the tests. Dr. Baker later came in carrying several tubes of integrated circuits. "Hey Annie, I just received chips from fabrication facilities in South Korea and France. You want to see if you can make these devices sing too" laughed Dr. Baker. "It would be my honor," replied Annie. "Did you observe any sound differences when you were testing the last batch of ICs" asked Dr. Baker? "Yes" replied Annie "specifically devices from different fabrication runs. I also noticed that the devices that had analog components embedded in them seemed to emit more lower frequencies. The pure digital devices generated more higher frequency information."

"The manager from the fabrication house in South Korea said he included a few devices whose internal architecture has been modified from the basic architecture. He said the functionality of the devices are the same, but these devices contain additional features to support another function." Annie said, "let me test these and I will see what happens. Hopefully I will be able to detect differences." "Thanks Annie," replied Dr. Baker. Annie began dismantling the previous devices she was testing. She was thinking about what a challenge it is going to be when trying to detect devices with altered architecture. "I sure like my job" said Annie to herself while smiling. "This is a cool project; I have got to make it work. Dr. Baker, I will get Jace to assist me with testing these new devices. I believe that he is up working in Dr. Sassenfeld's shop today. Is that okay with you?" "Sounds good Annie," said Dr. Baker.

It took several hours for Annie and Jace to set up the test jig to test the devices from South Korea. Once they had completed the test setup, Jace said "Hey Annie, which fab house are these devices from?" "They are from South Korea. The manager even threw in some devices whose architecture has been altered. The thought is that these devices might help us figure out how to detect altered devices." "Do you really think this is possible," asked Jace. "I mean, modern devices contain millions of transistors, if not more, and the noise generated by these devices is … switching chaotically … I just don't see how this can work." "You may be correct but let's give it a go …," said Annie."

It took a few more hours to get the test jigs setup and working properly. Annie and Jace began conducting pulse response tests. The waveform that Annie saw was what she had learned to expect. She told Jace about the artifacts they were seeing and what Dr. Baker had said might be of interest. Once they were able to get repeated tests working, Annie said, "I will contact Dr. Baker, he said he wants to be here when we start testing the devices with altered architecture."

Jace and Annie pulled another device out, the one with altered architecture. Dr. Baker arrived and he said, "Do you have the expected transient trace stored on the scope?" Jace said "yes". Dr. Baker said, "Ok, let's compare traces." Jace put both traces on the screen and they were identical. Dr. Baker and Annie looked intently at the traces. Annie made a lot of adjustments, but the traces were identical. The traces from the normal device and the one with the modified architecture were identical. Jace commented, "I know you guys had high hopes for this type of test, but I knew from the start that it would not be possible, there is just too much noise inside the chip to pull out any useful information. You guys need to stick with conventional and proven test methods." Dr. Baker looked at Annie and shook his head and said, "Jace, you are wrong …"

Right then, Jordan Pines from the budget office walked in and asked, "have you made any progress yet, we have a lot of money riding on this project." Dr. Baker calmly replied, "nothing yet"

That evening in France a text message arrived on Etienne's burner phone. It simply stated, "they are having no success, as predicted :)

7

Daniel and Josh were back at Los Campos eating their favorite meals with both red and green Chile. "This never gets old," said Daniel. Josh replied, "I didn't grow up eating Chile, especially green Chile rellenos but I sure love it now. I think it's fair to say that I am addicted." So, Josh, you asked me to lunch, what can I do for you." "It is probably nothing," said Josh "but Jordan, the budget guy, keeps showing up to the lab and asking weird questions. It just makes me feel uncomfortable, like he thinks I am doing something illegal or against policy. Annie and Jace were in the lab with me, and we were running pulse tests and he wanted to know whose devices we were testing. Why should that matter to him? Did you ever talk to him about coming into the lab unannounced?" "Yes, I did but I will talk to him again. Sorry, that happened. So how is the testing going? Anything to report yet." Josh replied, "Annie has some clever ideas to improve the test procedure and she started working on those ideas, Jace is more pessimistic about the test or at least the possibility that we can detect altered chip architectures. In fact, he doesn't think the test procedure can produce any valid results. Good thing he wasn't part of my Ph.D. committee," said Josh with a smile. Daniel looked at Josh and said, "he is just jealous, I think he wanted your job and has been a little resentful because he was not selected to run the project. He is a good engineer and is very thorough, he also used to work in a fab house before he came here so he has a lot of experience especially with testing devices. I think he is just one of those people who never believes that anyone can do something as well as himself. You ready to head back to work?" "Sure, thanks for talking to me, I appreciate it." said Josh.

When Josh got back to the lab, he could tell from the look on Annie's face that things weren't going well. "Dr. Baker, I am not sure what I am doing wrong concerning the devices from South Korea, I have not been able to distinguish between the devices with the normal architecture and the ones that have been altered, the transients look the same for both sets of devices and we know that they should be different … right, maybe Jace is right, it's too noisy of an environment, so what do we do now?"

Dr. Krist Hudson from the FBI's Cybersecurity division walked into the lab. "I hear you guys are making progress, can you provide me and my colleagues back in DC with an update." Josh took time to update Dr. Hudson on the current status of their work. "Dr. Hudson" said Josh, "we are currently looking at devices from South Korea and part of the lot contains devices with an altered architecture. We were hoping that there could be subtle differences in the transient response but so far, we have not had success." Dr. Hudson thought for a moment and said, "didn't you say earlier that you were hoping to identify a unique sound or feature that could indicate a change in the device?" "Yes, replied Josh, but unfortunately, we haven't identified any special features or signatures yet. I know we haven't demonstrated it yet, but my gut feeling is telling me that altered devices have to be emitting a unique signature when pulsed. I know this sounds like wishful thinking, but my research says this should happen." Dr. Hudson said, "let me call my colleagues back at the Hoover Building in DC and see if they have any recommendations." "Thanks," said Josh.

After Dr. Hudson left, Josh said, "Annie let's try a different technique on observing the transient current. Ask Jace if they have any high-resolution current probes somewhere in the lab that we could use. I want to try monitoring all available V_{DD} and ground connections on the ICs from South Korea. I just know that we should be seeing some differences in these devices. Thanks for checking on this. I am going to be in my office for the rest of the afternoon. I will check back with you tomorrow." Josh headed back to his office. After getting back to the office Josh called Ade "hey Ade, let's all go out for Italian food tonight at Lorenzo's, what do you think?" "Sounds good, oh by the way, have you been using the courting candle? You have been pretty occupied with your job", said Ade. "I don't want to be a single mom". Josh quietly said "you are right, sorry about that. I will be home at about 5:30.

Later that evening, the Baker family were all seated around a table at the restaurant. Josh ordered green Chile lasagna and Ade ordered spaghetti with meat sauce. Both kids ordered pizza. After their drinks arrived Josh said, "sorry again Ade for being so preoccupied with work, you know that you and our kids are the most important thing to me." Ade smiled, "I know that but remember, I don't plan to raise the kids by myself." With that comment Ade gently kicked Josh's leg under the table and raised her glass and smiled at Josh.

The Bakers were finishing up their supper when someone tapped Josh's shoulder, "hey Dr. Baker". Josh turned and noticed it was Jace from work. Josh said, "hey Jace, how are you. Oh, this is my wife Ade and our two kids, Sara and Sean." "Please to meet you, your husband is sure keeping us busy, oh Dr. Baker, I located the current probes you requested. They will be in the lab the first thing in the morning. It will be interesting to see if they make a difference. I will see you tomorrow" Jace turned and left, Josh looked at Ade and said, Jace is one of the engineers working on the project, I don't think he is really impressed with my approach and has said we are taking the wrong approach … enough of that, hey kids, how about ice cream afterwards, as long as your mom says okay." "The kids looked expectantly at their mom, and she said, "how about frozen custard from Caliches". Both kids said, "woo yummy". Ade smiled at Josh and reached for his hand and said, "Maybe you will get a treat tonight too." Josh just looked at Ade and smiled real big, kissed Ade's cheek and said, "thanks Ade, you always know what to say."

8

The next day Josh had renewed excitement about the project. Josh said, "ok, we have the current probes. Annie and Jace, take time to monitor the connection to all of the V_{DD} and ground rails. This device has 12 points to monitor, first run sample transient tests on the known good devices. I want to make sure that we are seeing correct information and we definitely have a clear picture of the transient." Annie jokingly remarks, "your excellency, is there anything else ...Dr. Baker." Josh turned to Annie and said, "sorry, just excited that we might get useful results today. I have got to prove this test procedure will work." Annie looked at Josh and says, "it will, just give us a few days." Jace just sat in the corner shaking his head and mumbled to himself, "this will never work."

They tested all of the ICs and then tested the devices from South Korea whose internal architecture had been altered. "What are we doing wrong? " exclaimed Josh. "This test should work. Annie, maybe we are not looking at a wide enough bandwidth. Let's alter the FFT and re-examine the devices." They made some adjustments and re-tested the devices but still no useful results. Josh looked at Jace and said, "Do you have any ideas?" Jace replied, "I told you guys that I didn't believe that this could work. It is just too noisy of an environment to get any useful results, sorry, I know you guys had high hopes but ...". Josh cutting off Jace's comments sarcastically replied, "thanks for your honest opinion."

Josh, after spending some time thinking, said, "let's try using a neural network algorithm to key on isolating unique features, let's first try a Denoising Artificial neural network. It does a good job of isolating features. I used artificial neural networks early in my Ph.D. work. Unfortunately, the test community was very reluctant to accept a procedure that was somewhat iffy, which I fully understand." Annie asked, "So how does the neural network learn or know what to look for?" Josh replied, you have to train the neural networks, this can be done by comparing a few known good devices with known bad or in this case devices with altered architecture. Then, you just let the computer spend a few hours or days going through a training phase. Basically, it's just adaptive statistical analysis. Once we complete the training phase then we should be able to insert another device and the neural network will simply tell us if the device is good or bad or if it has been altered based on its transient behavior. The bad part is it may take all night or longer to train the neural network." They set up the test jig, inserted a known good device, and ran a pulse test. They carefully examined the generated trace on the oscilloscope and saved the results. They then put a known altered device in the test jig, repeated the test, observed the resulting waveform, and saved it. Josh said, "We now have two unique waveforms stored, Annie, put these into the neural network, let it go through its training phase and then let it do it's magic. With that said, Annie pressed enter and two groups of numbers were being displayed on the screen. The two numbers displayed were basically the same. Josh said, "over time, the magnitude of the difference between the two numbers will be significantly different, indicating the neural network has identified unique differences between the devices. We will let the computers run overnight and then retest all of the devices from South Korea." And with the neural network being trained, Josh said, "I will see you guys back here in the morning."

Josh was first to arrive the next morning, he quickly checked the computer screen that was running the neural network. Two numbers were displayed;

$$0.1275 \qquad 0.9763$$

Josh smiled and said to himself, it looks like unique differences in the two devices had been identified. Right then, Annie and Jace walked into the lab. "Hey guys, it looks like the neural network successfully identified unique features between the two devices. Now we can run tests on all of the ICs and see how many altered devices will be identified.

Jace and Annie began laying out all of the devices to be tested. Josh said, "hey guys, I have a sheet that shows which devices have or have not had their internal architecture altered. Remember, it is important that we try to run a **blind test,** we don't want to know if a device is good or has been altered prior to running the test. We will use the sheet to verify our results when we complete the testing." Jace and Annie both said, "sounds good, we will mix up the devices before starting the tests."

The devices were carefully laid out and Jace and Annie began testing each of the devices. The first device tested came back with a score of 0.113. The next device had a score of 0.132. The third device had a score of 0.972. Josh smiled and said, "this is how it is supposed to work, we are getting distinct grouping of the test results. Let's go ahead and finish testing the devices." The majority of the scores for the tested devices were close to either 0.12 or 0.97. Two of the devices produced scores of about 0.45. Josh told Jace and Annie that his research showed that devices that didn't clearly classify probably had some abnormal properties, possibly containing a defect. I actually did some research work for a National Lab trying to show that this technique could be used to detect defects. We had limited success, but it did work, better than a coin toss. In the academic world that is considered a step forward, but it is not sufficient for industry."

With all of the devices fully tested, Josh pulled out the paperwork that showed if the device was normal or if its internal architecture had been altered. Josh, Jace, and Annie examined the list and compared the scores of the pulse tests for the devices. Annie excitedly said, "we have properly classified all of the devices except for the two devices with scores of about 0.45. This is exciting!" Jace spoke up and said, "I am surprised…" Annie spoke up and said, "yes, but it worked. We were able to properly classify most of the devices." "And we detected devices with altered device architecture!" Josh said.

"This is exciting!" Josh exclaimed, "this proves the technique works". "But does this technique work when you don't know if any of the devices have altered architecture," said Jace. "In the real world you won't have samples of devices with altered architecture, then what do you do". "Jace, don't be so negative, let's enjoy the moment", said Annie, "we will figure it out, right Dr. Baker". Josh looked at everyone and said, "I certainly hope so, I'm going home and celebrate with Ade and kids and enjoy the moment. See both of you in the morning ".

The next morning, Josh found a note on his door that said, "mandatory meeting at 8:00 in the conference room for you and all members of your group. *JP*" Josh turned to head to the conference room when he ran into Jace and Annie just arriving at the lab. "Hey, we have been summoned to the conference room by the budget guy, Jordan Pines. I am not sure what is going on…" said Josh.

They arrived in the conference room, Jordan greeted them as they entered. Dr. Rico, Sassenfeld, and Hudson were also there. Josh, Annie, and Jace sat down and Jordan said, "Thanks for coming everyone. There is an important development that needs your attention. Dr. Hudson from the FBI's Cyber Security has an important issue to discuss with you."

"Thanks," said, Dr. Hudson. It has come to our attention that devices with compromised ICs have been shipped. We only know that it is coming from a fabrication facility in Europe. Our source says that the devices have an altered architecture, and the modified devices are capable of transmitting compromised information to a server on the dark web. I am here today to get an update from you, can you comment on your progress Dr. Baker."

"As of yesterday, we successfully identified devices with an altered internal architecture. We had about a 95% success rate, the caveat is that we did have knowledge of a known good device and an altered device. We used that device knowledge to train a neural network." Annie spoke up and said, "we are seeing differences, there is definitely something there, we just have to have a properly trained neural network." "Dr. Baker, based on your experience, will you be able to detect altered devices from other fabrication facilities or will you have to retrain your neural network?" asked Dr. Hudson. "Based on our success yesterday, I am confident we will have success, as for retraining the neural network, I don't know yet, but my guess is yes, we will have to retrain the neural net, but what we will learn in the process will make it easier to test other devices," replied Dr. Baker. "That's good, I have arranged additional shipments of devices for your team to test, which is why I asked Jordan Pines to set up this meeting. Your team is going to be very busy for the next few months and you are going to need additional funding for testing, supplies, and staff. I will meet with you and your team tomorrow to discuss logistics. Are there any questions? If not, then that is it for today. Thank you.

Jordan spoke up and said, "I will be contacting you Dr. Baker, and your supervisor, Dr. Rico to discuss changes with your task order and the new funding. Please contact me if you have any questions and please, keep me updated on the status of the project." "Jace, with the task order change, you will be assigned to Dr. Baker's group until further notice," said Dr. Rico. Jace smiled and said, "glad to help".

Josh, Annie, and Jace went back to the lab, Josh jokingly said to Jace, "welcome to the team." Addressing both Jace and Annie, "I have got to do some thinking before we start the new phase of testing. This is getting interesting, but I am not sure about training or retraining the neural network. Let me know if you guys have any thoughts."

That evening in France a text message arrived on Etienne's burner phone. It stated, "*they suspect that the altered devices are coming from Europe but they don't know any more than that. They haven't tested our devices yet.*"

A little while later, a text message arrived on a burner phone at ESL. The text message stated, *keep me updated, understand …*

On Etienne's burner phone the message simply said, *understood.*

9

The next morning, Josh arrived at the lab to find Annie already at work. "Hey Annie" said Josh, "glad to see you are already here. What are you working on?" Annie replied, "I am researching neural networks. I didn't study these in grad school, I am just trying to keep up with things. Right at that moment, Jace came in, looking a little haggard. Josh said, "what happened to you, looks like you had a tough night." Jace replied, "yes, just a lot on my mind, I will be okay. "Everyone, come over here, I want to discuss something," said Josh.

Annie and Jace gathered around Josh, and he said, "I have been thinking about our next steps. What we have successfully shown is that we are able to detect devices with altered architecture. The devices we tested from South Korea proved this. This is a very good thing however, we had to have examples of both types of devices for the neural network to fully converge to a solution." "And to be fully trained," said Annie. "You are correct but the situation now, in the real world, is we don't know what devices are good and which devices have been altered." Annie and Jace looked at Josh and Annie said, "So where do we go from here?" Josh thought for a moment and said, "for the devices from South Korea, we know the good devices and we also know the altered devices. Let's try retraining our neural network using only one device from the South Korean lot, we can select a good or an altered device for training. We will get the training score down to less than 0.1." Annie spoke up and said, "that will require deep learning." "Very good Annie, that is exactly correct and what are the issues that we will face." Annie thought for a moment and said, "one, we have to modify the feedback and feedforward paths in the neural network and two, it is going to take longer times to fully train the network.

Jace and Annie began randomly setting out all the devices. Josh spoke up, "remember, we cannot know if a device is good or altered. We will evaluate everything once we complete the training and testing." Annie spoke up and said, "this is exciting, I hope we have luck." Jace replied, "I wish I was as optimistic as you and Dr. Baker. I am not sure this can work, I mean how can an artificial neural network do magic. How can anyone possibly know if a device is good or altered by pulsing the power supply, this is not a magic show." "Jace", Josh replied, "I can ask Dr. Rico to replace you if you feel this is a waste of your time." "I am sorry, I just had a tough night, I guess I am just grumpy. No, I want to monitor ... be involved with this project, sorry.

They randomly selected one of the devices, ran the pulse test and stored the waveform. Annie and Josh completed work on the computer making changes to the neural network, preparing it for deep learning. Josh turned to Annie and Jace and said, "What we are going to try to do is deep training on the one device we have randomly selected. We need to get the score for the neural network down to 0.03 or lower. Once again, the goal is that we will have a neural network that will be able to detect an altered device. I expect the scores for altered devices to be 0.1 or higher. This is just my gut feeling. Any score significantly higher than 0.03 is enough for us to get suspicious." Jace spoke up and said, "I would think that the scores for every device would be radically different, regardless if the device has been altered. Just my opinion." Josh said, "I have tested thousands of devices and good devices tend to produce very similar transient currents when pulsed. The exception we saw was when a device had a defect or was actually bad." "What if we select a device that has an altered architecture for training the neural network. Won't that negate or skew the results? How will this affect the scores?" asked Jace. Josh replied, "what I would expect is that other altered devices will generate a similar score to the original altered device used for training. Good or normal devices should generate high scores. The problem I am seeing is that we will be showing that we are detecting differences in the devices but we have not definitively identified altered devices, just that the devices are different. In the meantime, let's go ahead and start deep learning of the neural network to get ready for testing the devices. Annie, can you come to my office, I want to discuss our next step with you."

Josh and Annie adjourned to his office and Josh said, "I appreciate your initiative to learn more about neural networks. Let's look at where we are now, we have demonstrated that we can detect that a device has been altered. We have transient current waveforms for those devices with altered architecture. What I want you to do is analyze those waveforms and see if you can find some feature or artifact within the transients that are unique that we could possibly use to detect altered devices. This is not an easy task, I spent a couple of years trying to find something unique, but never had success, but now we a a a set of unique transient waveforms, courtesy of the fab in South Korea for us to play with, what do you think? Annie smiled really big and said, "I will get started on it this afternoon." "Annie, let's keep this just among us okay..." Annie smiled and gave two thumbs up, "you've got it boss!"

Right then, Jordan Pines walked into Josh's office and said, "Well, what's up with the project. Can you detect altered devices yet? There is a lot of money riding on your success, guys." "Jordan, you need to be talking to Dr. Rico to get updates on the project, he and I are talking regularly about the project, OK...". "Alright, I will talk with Dr. Rico, I don't know why you are so evasive and secretive. We all know what you have been tasked to do." With that, Jordan exited Josh's office. "Sorry for that interruption Annie, thanks for your support! We'll talk more tomorrow.

Annie left Josh's office, entered the lab and immediately Jace said, "So what are you guys planning that's so secretive, how come I am not included?" "Jace, Dr. Baker was just giving me my next task, I am sure he is going to do that with you too.' said Annie, "you've also been somewhat of a jerk about everything …. what is up with you and this project, everything seems so personal to you. You need to lighten up …". Jace dropped his head and just walked out. Annie just shook her head and went back to reading a scholarly publication on deep learning with neural networks.

10

That evening, Josh, Ade, and the kids went out to eat Italian food. Josh had his usual green Chile lasagna, Ade had spaghetti with meat sauce and of course, the kids ordered pizza. Ade was telling Josh about the latest collectible she had found at the local thrift store. "I found an old spinning wheel, in excellent shape. It lists on eBay for $200.00 and I got it for $45.00." "That's great", said Josh, "where are you going to put it?" Ade, replied grinning, "don't know yet, but I will find a place. I also found a wooden wheel from a Model T Ford. It is waaay cool, I already found a place for it in the backyard." Josh replied jokingly, "you actually found a place for it, our back yard already has quite a few things." Ade smiled and said, "you can never have too many collectibles, they are an important part of history and educating our children. Just Think of it, how many kids know what a Betty lamp is. Our kids are very special. You remember what our daughter said the other day, you can't have too many antiques. Our daughter is obviously advanced for her age and has her priorities correct." Josh said, "you are so correct, she is very special, she has the gift of words ... we are lucky parents. I am a lucky guy too. Thank you." "Let's see if you say that after you see our credit card, Ade said sheepishly as she reached for Josh's hand.

Right then a man walked up to Josh and Ade. "Hello Josh". It was Jordan, the budget guy from work. "I see you are hard at work," Jordan said laughingly. Josh was a little surprised but said, "Hi Jordan, this is my wife Ade." Ade shook Jordan's hand and Jordan said, "I have seen you at the local garage sales. I try to find things but I am not always successful. How about you, find anything interesting". "Quelques trésors pour le jardin" said Ade in French. (*some treasures for the yard*). Jordan looked at Ade and replied, "tres bien, c'est amusant oui." (Very good, it is fun, yes). Ade smiled and replied, "you are correct and your French is excellent." "Thanks" replied Jordan, "I spent a few years in France working on a project, got the opportunity to practice French and enjoy the cuisine. ". Where did you work?" Asked Josh. "I worked at a semiconductor manufacturing facility, outside Paris. With that, Jordan said, "see you at work tomorrow, Josh, nice meeting you Ade." and he left their table.

Ade said, "he seems like a nice guy, but my first impression of him at the garage sales was that he is sort of creepy and borderline obnoxious. I have seen him at several garage sales the last few weeks. Never saw him before that …. ". "Yes, he is kind of creepy at work too," said Josh. "Sometimes I do not know where he is coming from. He can act like your best friend one moment and a very grumpy and borderline hysterical manager the next. Hey, how was your supper?" "Tres excelente," replied Ade, I also spent time in Paris until some guy I met in college made me move to the U.S." "C'est dommage, n'est pas" (That's too bad, isn't it.) And I thought I rescued you from Roswell, not France, said Josh smiling. "C'est possible, peut-être que tu m'as séduit. [It is possible, maybe you seduced me]." "Oui madame, je suis ashamed. Peux-tu Jamal's me perdonner" [Yes mam, I am ashamed. Can you ever forgive me]. Ade replied, "I will forgive you later" as she kicked Josh's leg under the table. "Merci, m'dame. [Thank you ma'am]

11

The next morning, Josh arrived at work excited to see what his group could accomplish. He was very anxious to find out how the neural network had done. The concept of doing deep learning fascinated him. Josh found Annie sitting at the computer. She smiled at Josh and said, "hey Dr. Baker, the network has trained down to a score of 0.028, what do you think?" turning the computer monitor so Josh could see the screen. "This is great," Josh said. Jace. came into the lab and said, "how are the neural nets doing today?" He obviously was in better shape than yesterday, and he had a smile on his face. "Glad to see you in good spirits today," said Josh. "Let's get out the devices from South Korea and rerun the pulse tests using the newly trained neural network."

Annie and Jace began setting up the equipment so that they could begin testing. Jace placed one of the devices in the test jig, Annie made adjustments on the equipment and they ran a test. Annie took the data from the pulsed waveform and put it into the neural network, pressed enter and said, "here we go." Within a few seconds, the screen displayed a score of 0.025. Josh said, let's try another device. They set up everything, ran another test and put the data into the trained neural network. This one produces a score of 0.031. Josh looked at the screen and said, "Well, at least it produces consistent results, but we still don't know if this is a good device or an altered one. Guys let's try another one. The easy thing would be to test all of the devices right away, but I like the suspense. Ok, let's try another one." Annie and Jace repeated the test, input the pulsed data into the neural network and waited for the resulting score. The computer screen displayed 0.821. Annie yelled out, "we got 0.821 Dr. Baker!" Josh smiled and pulled out the list he had for the ICs indicating whether the device was good or altered. Josh smiled really big and said, "my sheet indicates that this is an altered device and the previous two devices are good devices. "Annie, Jace, it looks like the deep training of the neural network is working! Let's go ahead and test the rest of the devices. Make sure you don't check the status of the devices until all have been tested. I know I am being paranoid, but the academic part of me wants to make sure our results are not skewed or contaminated. Do you guys understand?" Annie and Jace both said, "we understand you *jefe*." Josh just snickered and said, "thanks guys…"

Annie and Jace began testing the remaining devices. The data from each pulsed waveform was input into the neural network and the generated scores began to get displayed. When they were done, Annie said, "I wrote some code last night that will make it easy for us to view the results. The results are displayed in table form, making it easier to view and analyze the test results." Annie pressed a few keystrokes and a table of results were displayed. "I also set up the table so it displays the results, sorted by magnitude."

Project: *Pulse Response Tests / J.Baker*   **Task order: 903213**
South Korea Devices   **June 12, 2022**

1. 0.018	11. 0.52	16. 0.81
2. 0.019	12. 0.61	17. 0.821
3. 0.020	13. 0.63	18. 0.935
4. 0.025	14. 0.725	19. 0.937
5. 0.031	15. 0.78	20. 0.955
6. 0.0689		21. 0.962

7. 0.171		22. 0.971
8. 0.19		23. 0.975
9. 0.221		24. 0.988
10. 0.32		25. 0.99

"This is excellent Annie." Josh said. Annie, Jace, and Josh looked at the results. Jace said, "there somewhat appears to be a natural grouping of the scores, but some scores like for devices 11 to 15 appear somewhat questionable." Josh spoke up and said, "I have conducted thousands of pulse tests and there have always been outliers, just like what we are seeing right now. Devices 1 to 10 look like they match up or belong to the same group. This is also true for devices 16 to 25 which have a similar type of grouping with their scores. Devices 10 to 15, who knows. let's go ahead and review the paperwork on these devices and see which of these devices are good devices or if their architecture has been altered."

Josh pulled out the paperwork and said, "ok, this is it ….. Device #1 - Good, Device#2 - Good, Device#3 - Good." The group began to get a little excited and gave each other high fives." "Devices 4-13 are also good. Device 14 has altered architecture, device 15 - Good, and Devices 16 to 25 have altered architecture.

We'll team, it appears that we might have found a way to detect devices with altered architecture. Right then, Dr. Rico and Jordan Pines stepped into the lab. "Hello Dr. Baker, sorry for the interruption, we are just checking on the status of the project," said Dr. Rico. "Have you made any progress Dr. Baker?" asked Jordan. "I have repeatedly told you that there is a lot of money riding on this, and your reputation." "Jordan, lighten up", said Dr. Rico. "Whatever", commented Jordan.

"So, what is the status, Dr. Baker?" asked Dr. Rico. "We have tested the 25 devices from South Korea and we successfully classified or identified 19 of 25 devices giving us a success rate of …, what does that come out to be Annie?" "That would be 76%, Dr. Baker." "The result is that we have demonstrated that we can differentiate most of the good devices from devices with altered architecture, of course in this case we knew we had devices with altered architecture, but we were very careful to not bias or skew our results. We are confident we are on the right track."

That sounds great Dr. Baker, please keep me posted. Jordan, do you have any questions?" asked Dr. Rico. "Yes, have you tested any devices from Italy or France yet, just curious." "No" said Dr. Baker, "the devices from Italy are scheduled to arrive next week, the devices from France are here but we have not tested them. We have been focused on the devices from South Korea, trying to validate our testing methodology. I will keep Dr. Rico advised on the project status." Jordan replied, "Let me know when you are testing the devices from France, I used to work at the fab in Corbeil-Essonnes you know, I guess that I have some emotional attachment to that place, you know, I was there for two years." Josh replied, "I will keep Dr. Rico advised." Jordan and Dr. Rico turned to leave, Dr. Rico said to Josh, "sorry for the interruption, thank you for the project update, thanks again." "Thank you both for stopping by," said Josh.

After Dr. Rico and Jordan left, Josh asked Annie and Jace to sit and talk. "Just recapping the status of the project, based on the tests we just completed on the South Korean devices and using deep learning of the neural network, we successfully demonstrated that we have a fair chance of detecting devices with altered architecture. We need to investigate how we might be able to increase that percentage. Any thoughts?"

Jace spoke up first, "guys, I know I have been less than civil with you when discussing this project. I want to say right now that I am very impressed with the results. I never thought this would work, but you have surprised me. Once again, my apologies to both of you. I will do my best to provide better support in the future." "Thanks, Jace," said both Josh and Annie. "Let's call it a day, see you Monday." said Josh. "We will start work on the devices from France on Monday, everyone have a good evening and weekend." "Thanks", said both Annie and Jace as Josh left the lab. "Hey Annie, would you like to go get a beer and some food?" said Jace.

"Sounds good, where do you want to meet up?" Said Annie. "Let's try The Venue, they have many beers on tap and the "Bats" are incredible." said Jace. "I know it is a Sports Bar but what the heck are Bats?" asked Annie? Jace replied, "they are made with Hatch Green Chile encrusted in diced pecans and then deep fried, it is heaven. My ex-girlfriend used to really love them and me but … she found …. someone else a few weeks ago. That is why I have been so moody." "Sorry about that Jace, let's go to The Venue, get some beers and an order of Bats, on me." said Annie. "Thanks Annie, I will meet you there in 15 minutes."

The atmosphere at The Venue was what Jace was hoping for, good music playing in the bar, the sounds of many people enjoying a break from work or school and the perfect time and place to be with a friend. Jace and Annie found a good place to sit at The Venue, sitting across from each other in a booth. "Thanks, Jace for the invite, this is nice." "Wait til you try the Bats, you will fall in love with them" said Jace. Annie looked at Jace and noticed he had tears in his eyes. Annie took a deep breath and said, "I am very sorry Jace". She reached across the table and grabbed Jace's hand. Jace was surprised but smiled, "thanks Annie … you are a good friend. Did you need to call your boyfriend and ask him to join us?" Annie laughed, "That's sort of personal …. No, I am not seeing anyone right now" she said with a sheepish grin. As she looked at Jace she realized he is actually a nice looking guy and he is being really sweet. Jace was looking at Annie too and said to her, "you are kinda cute when you are not being so serious." Annie laughed and said "What a nice thing to say to a girl … I think." Annie reached across the table and grabbed Jaces's hand and said, "let's order those beers and Bats before things get too weird." Jace squeezed Annie's hand and says, "got it."

After a couple of beers and orders of the Bats, Annie said, "So what happened with you and your ex-girlfriend, … if you don't mind me asking." Jace replied, "I always suspected she didn't like engineers. No, seriously, I guess it just ran its course, she is focused on her music, and I guess I am focused on my current job. …… no, don't say it, I know I haven't been the best employee or co-worker these past few weeks. I might have been envious of Josh, I mean, …. Dr. Baker for getting the job," he said with a smile. "I applied for the job too, but …. I know he is more qualified; he does have a Ph.D. and he does know how to test and evaluate integrated circuits at a level I have never done and the use of neural networks and deep learning are pretty clever. I was also hoping to get the position and get a pay raise. I have gotten myself into a financial situation which is tough." "Sorry about that," said Annie. "Is it bad, do you have a big debt?" said Annie. "No, it's under control, I have been doing some sort of consulting that has put me in a better financial situation. Hey, I have had a really fun time tonight, thanks for agreeing to meet me here" said Jace. "I have had a nice time too and thanks for sharing about your breakup, we all have had similar drama in our lives" replied Annie.

"Hey, I'm going to attend the Whole Enchilada Festival tomorrow? I am going with my sister and her husband; it should be a lot of fun. Are you going?" Jace replied, "No, I will probably stay at home." Annie quickly said, bumping Jace's side, "Why don't you come with us, it will be fun." "Are you sure?" Asked Jace. "Of course, you are kind of fun when you're not grumpy. So do you want to go?" Asked Annie. "Thanks Annie, sure, that does sound like fun, what time and where should I meet you?" "Let's meet at the Sprouts parking lot at 11:30. We will probably eat at the festival and maybe we will come back to The Venue for beer and Bats. I think I am hooked" said Annie with a big smile. Annie and Jace walked to the parking lot and Annie said, "Thank you for inviting me, Jace, I had a lot of fun tonight, the 'Bats' are heavenly, and you are not too bad either." She looked up at Jace and smiled really big, gave Jace a hug and kissed his cheek. Jace smiled and said, "I had a nice time too, see you at the Sprouts parking lot at 11:30 tomorrow."

12

Josh, Jace, and Annie all arrived at the lab about the same time. Josh said, "Great to see everyone, I hope you had a good weekend." Josh noticed that Annie and Jace both grinned and Jace said, "Had a great weekend Dr. Baker, ready to help you in whatever way I can." "Me too!" said Annie. Josh just looked at both of them and said, "Ok guys, what's going on?" Annie quickly said, "nothing, just had a nice weekend with friends." "Same with me," said Jace. "Ok, maybe someday you will let in on your secret," said Josh. "Let's start setting up the test jigs to test the devices from France. I believe that there are twenty-five devices. Of course, we don't know the status of any of the devices, we will just randomly select one device to be used for deep learning of the neural net."

"Annie, make sure the neural net is ready to run and Jace, select one device for us to do deep learning with. Go ahead and run a pulse test and have that data ready for Annie to run when the neural network is ready for training. I am going to step out a minute to talk with Dr. Rico." Josh exited the lab and Annie started giggling. "I think Dr. Baker suspects something, how could he know we got together this weekend? Hey Jace …., I really had a nice time, thanks." "I had lots of fun too" said Jace, "you are definitely full of surprises. What are you doing tonight?" Annie replied, "Oh, I have a supper date, how about you?" Jace replied, "That's funny, me too, maybe we will run into each other." They both looked at each other and smiled really big, Annie bumped Jace's hip with hers and said, "I did have a lot of fun." Jace smiled and said, "Me too!"

Josh knocked on Dr. Rico's door. "Hey Josh, come on in, I am just visiting with Jordan, what's up?" Josh noticed that Jordan was seated in the room across from Daniel's desk. "Hi, Jordan," said Josh. "Daniel, I just wanted to update you on the project. We are starting the tests on the devices from France today. It will take at least a full day to fully train the neural net." "How many devices are you using in your training?" asked Dr. Rico. "We are using just one device and we are doing deep learning." "Remind me again what deep learning of neural networks are." said Dr. Rico.

Josh said, "Deep learning with neural networks is commonly used in self-driving vehicles, pattern recognition, deep neural networks can have hundreds of hidden layers. The challenge is that these types of networks can take a long time to train, requiring a lot of processing time to get them ready for use." "Why do you need to use neural nets?" asked Dr. Rico. Josh replied, "The waveform we are analyzing is just too complex for normal pattern recognition techniques, there are too many variables to deal with, neural networks just seem like the best method. Conventional testing techniques are fine when you need to track specific metrics, but in our case, we don't have specific metrics for these altered devices. We don't even know which devices have been altered. The deep learning is going to enable us to detect altered architectures and solve our problems, …. I hope."

"Josh, give me your honest opinion, do you think this is going to work?" Asked Dr. Rico. "I believe that it will" said Josh, "but it's not going to be easy, Annie and Jace have been providing me with great support and critical review. So far, we have been able to adapt to the challenges we have faced, and we have successfully modified our test approach to provide the results we are looking for." "In all honesty, that sounds like boilerplate language people use when they aren't sure where their work is headed," said Dr. Rico. "Try that answer again." "Daniel, in all honesty, I don't know. I want to say yes but … we are having to modify our test approach for every group of devices we evaluate. We keep making changes, thinking this will be the correct technique to evaluate the devices but, the next lot comes in and we end up having to make additional changes. Basically, we then have to start over. We will start evaluating the devices from France tomorrow, but we don't know if there are any altered devices in that group. The group of devices from South Korea included sample devices with altered architecture which enabled us to mostly isolate good and altered devices. We are just starting to get things set up so we can evaluate the French devices today, I will advise you about their status by Wednesday." "Thanks for the honesty and stopping by, I will follow up with you on Wednesday." said Daniel. "Thanks, Daniel, see you Wednesday." Josh acknowledged Jordan and left the room.

Josh got back to the lab, a little confused about the meeting with Daniel. Why was Jordan in Daniel's office? That guy keeps showing up, it seems like he should be in his own office working. I have got to let it go, Josh thought, I have too many other things to worry about, like how we are going to test the new devices from France.

"Hey Jace, Annie. Let's get set up to start testing a device from the fab in France. Just randomly select one device, capture the pulse response and then begin training the neural network. Annie, let's shoot for a training score of 0.03 or lower. Once again, I expect the computer will have to run all night." Annie and Jace quickly began getting things setup. About 30 minutes later, Annie said, "We have successfully captured the Pulse Response from the sample device. Dr. Baker, would you like to examine the waveform?" asked Annie. Josh examined the waveform and said, "It looks similar to the other devices we have tested, however, there is some interesting artifact resting on the waveform that I didn't see with the South Korean devices. I am not sure what it is, it may just be something unique to the fab in France. Annie, let's go ahead and start training the neural network." Annie entered some data into the computer, pressed the enter key and said, "Ok, training has started, we will check on it in the morning."

Josh said, "Let's start getting ready for the devices from Italy. They are scheduled to arrive this week. Jace, make sure we have the latest data sheets for these devices."

That evening in France another text message arrived on Etienne's burner phone. It stated, *things are getting a little uneasy, they plan to start testing our devices on Wednesday. I will carefully monitor their results and I will know more in two days. Oh, FYI, they are also using some kind of deep learning technique and neural networks.*

13

That evening, Ade was drinking a beer and Josh had a glass of wine. Josh said, "Do you ever think it's weird that I drink wine and you drink beer, and you are from France." Ade laughed and said, no, I just know what I like, I prefer to think that I have evolved and you ... you are just special. So, what's up with work?" asked Ade. "It's going okay," said Josh, "I'm just not happy with some of the politics at work. The bosses seem to be fairly happy, but the budget guy still irritates me. I went to see Daniel today and that guy was in his office. He didn't say anything but, ... I don't know, he is making me uncomfortable. Probably just my imagination ...". "No, his mannerisms at garage sales make me uncomfortable too." said Ade. "He acts like everyone should get out of his way. This weekend at a garage sale, I was looking at an item, I asked about purchasing it and then he proceeded to pick it up and said he wanted to buy it, he just took it from me. He is a very rude person; I hate it when people do that." "Sorry that happened to you, don't people know that you are a serious tiquer and you have to keep updating your inventory." Josh said smiling. Ade gently kicked Josh's leg, "Be kind, garage sales can be stressful. Do you know what it is like for someone else to get that special item you have been looking for and do you know what it is like to finally find that special item and someone else tells the seller that I am not interested, arrg. It makes me angry, but not enough to stop 'junking'." Josh smiled at Ade and said, "You know, you are special and beautiful, I am sorry people get ugly at garage sales, they shouldn't do that to you. How was school for the kids today? "They both have math homework, I told them that Dad will help them with it tonight," said Ade. "Of course, I will help them, I hope I remember how to solve the problems though," said Josh. "The Ph.D. did sort of drain my brain of any practical knowledge. Good thing you handle the finance's, sometimes, I am still not thinking clearly.

Josh arrived at work the next morning to find Jace and Annie drinking coffee and looking at the computer screen. "What's up guys", asked Josh. Jace said, "you told Annie to train the neural network down to a score of 0.03 or less but it seems to be stuck at 0.45. Does that make sense? Do you have a recommendation?" Josh thought for a moment and said, "I hate wasting a day but let's retest the device and generate a new pulse response test". "Hey Josh, remember that weird artifact on the pulse response we saw yesterday, could that be causing the problem." asked Annie. "I was thinking that the artifact could be a way of detecting something, I am not sure what though." said Josh. "Right now, the big concern is to figure out why the neural network is not converging to a solution. Let's generate a new pulse response, put the data into the neural network and let the computer and software do their magic."

Jace and Annie proceeded to run the new test and when they were done, they input the data into the neural network. Annie pressed enter on the computer keyboard and numbers began to appear on the screen. "We will let this run all night and hopefully we can take measurements tomorrow", said Josh. "We received 25 devices from a U.S. based fabrication facility this morning, let's get setup to begin testing of these devices too." Annie asked, "What steps will we take for the U.S. devices?" "Josh replied, "Let's plan on just selecting one device for deep learning of the neural network. Once the network has been trained, then we will evaluate the remaining devices. Hopefully, we will have better luck with these devices than what we are having with the devices from France."

Jace and Annie began setting up all of the test gear to get ready for the U.S. devices. The current probes had to be attached to the test jig, complete the setup, inserted a device and ran a pulse test just to verify that it is working properly. Annie and Jace examined the generated waveform. Annie said, "After looking at these a few times, I am beginning to recognize similar behavior, I guess that my internal neural network is getting trained." Jace just laughed, and thought to himself, how cute and said, "Hey Annie, would you like to maybe go out to eat tonight". "Sure," replied Annie, "Where do you want to go?" "How about La Posta in Mesilla," said Jace "and then we can walk the Plaza and visit some of the stores." "Sounds good Jace."

Josh received a call, it was Dr. Rico. "Daniel, what can I do for you, …. sure, I can come down, I will be there in about ten minutes. Josh put away his phone and said to Annie and Jace, "I will be at Dr. Rico's office for a little bit," and he walked out of the office. When Josh arrived at the office, he found the FBI guy, Dr. Hudson sitting in the office with Daniel. "Hi Josh, please come in and shut the door." Josh sat down and said, "what's up". "Josh, we have an important update from the FBI. Dr. Hudson, please tell Josh what you told me."

"Our security guys from the FBI and guys from the NSA have uncovered some unusual text message traffic from somewhere in France and somebody here at ESL. We have not been able to narrow the search. We suspect they are using burner phones to send the messages, but we are not sure. The messages seem to be addressing the testing of the devices from France. They know when you are scheduled to test the devices and they even mentioned that you are using neural networks for analyzing the pulse response. We just want you to be aware of the situation, we don't have specific threats targeting you or your staff or your lab. Just try to be a little more careful. I have arranged to have one of our guys shadow you at work, you already know him, it's Jace, he actually a special consultant to the FBI. He is well trained and can deal with any threats that might surface." Dr. Rico spoke up and said, "I have alerted the security staff for our building, and they will be stepping up security, in particular for your lab. We don't have any information that says your family needs to take special precautions, but just make sure you and your family are careful when you leave your house.,

Josh just stared at the two gentlemen, "Thanks for making me aware of the situation, wow, this is a little unnerving. We started testing the devices from France today, we don't have any results yet and don't expect to have any until Wednesday or Thursday. Do you really think this has something to do with our testing of the devices from France?" Dr. Hudson said, "We don't actually know for sure; we only know that the message traffic is between France and someone at ESL. We just want you to be cautious. Here is my card with my direct phone number, call it anytime day or night." "Ok, thanks for making me aware of the situation. Can I discuss this with Annie and Jace?" "Yes", said both Daniel and Dr. Hudson. Dr. Hudson added, "Jace has already been briefed and he fully understands the situation." "Thanks, can I go back to the lab now unless you have something else?" Dr. Rico spoke up and said, "Josh, sorry this is happening, just watch your back." "Thanks, said Josh as he exited the office. Josh got back to the lab and said, "guys, we need to talk."

14

Jace was the first to speak, "So what's up Josh?" "Apparently there is text message chatter going on between someone in France and someone at ESL. I was meeting with Dr. Rico and also Dr. Hudson from the FBI, Jace, I guess you already knew that." said Josh. "Jace, would you like to say something?" Jace smiled and said, "Yes, my name really is Jace and I am a special consultant with the FBI. I am here to assist with trying to locate devices with altered architecture. I have a master's degree in Electrical Engineering in VLSI Design and I am trying my best to support what you both are trying to accomplish. I had my doubts early on, but you have convinced me that I was operating with blinders on. What you have been able to accomplish so far is incredible. Annie, your contribution to deep learning is also remarkable. I am happy to be part of this." "Jace," Josh said, "Thanks for bringing us up to date, I have to ask, are you here to protect us or the devices?" Jace replied, "Originally, my task was to monitor the devices coming into the lab, but I like working with you guys. Annie, you are becoming very special to me." Annie just looked at Jace but didn't say anything. "I will do everything I can to make sure you are both safe,' said Jace. "Thanks," said Josh, "Ok guys, let's get back to work."

Josh got very serious and said, "Ok, we have 25 devices from the U.S. fab house. We don't know anything about these devices except the pin assignments and power supply connections. Jace, select one of the devices to be used for training. We can only assume that all of the devices are normal, and none have an altered architecture." "Are you okay Dr. Baker?" asked Annie. Josh just shook his head and said, "I am okay, I am just a little concerned about Ade and our kids. I am used to dealing with unreasonable demands from faculty and bosses but potential threats from the 'bad guys' are a little unsettling. Do you have any suggestions Jace, you have been very quiet?" Jace was looking at the ground. He raised his head and said, "Sorry, no I am just as much concerned about this as you are. Our intel indicated we had a little more time to get ready, but things are moving fast now. As I said earlier, I promise I will do everything I can to make sure both of you are safe and Dr. Baker, we will look out for your family too."

Jace went on describing what steps are being put in place by the building security. "We already have twenty-four hour security and video monitoring for all entrances and hallways. We also have additional security in the parking garage. As for the devices that have already been tested or the devices currently being tested, make sure these are put into the safe when not being used."

"Annie," said Jace "Here is the data from the pulse test for the U.S. device." Annie entered the data into the computer and pressed enter to start the deep learning for the neural network. "We should have results by sometime tomorrow afternoon." Josh thanked everyone and said, "What a day, I didn't see this coming. Let's go home early today, I need to give my family a hug." Annie and Jace both said, "We will see you tomorrow." "Annie," said Jace. "Are you still up for going out to eat?" "Yes, Jace, but we need to have a serious discussion tonight. I will be ready by 6:00 since we are leaving work early. With that said, Annie walked quickly out of the lab.

Josh's wife was very surprised when he walked into the front door of his home. "What are you doing home so early," said Ade. Josh carefully looked at Ade and said, "There is a situation at work that I need to discuss with you. Apparently, some 'bad guys' out of France are collaborating with someone at ESL. I had a discussion with Dr. Rico and the FBI rep this morning and they have recommended that

I be very careful. They are not sure if there is immediate danger, but I was told to be cautious. The FBI guy's name is Dr. Hudson and here is his business card. He said you can call him anytime, day or night if you have concerns." Ade looked carefully at Josh and said, "This is not good. Josh, what about our kids, are they in any danger?" "Ade, maybe you and the kids should go to Grandma's house in Roswell until this situation gets resolved." "Josh, this is crazy …." After a long pause, Ade said, you are right, I will call work and tell them the situation. Josh, what about you, are you okay?" asked Ade. They have put in additional security for our building and my lab. I will be okay, oh that guy from work you met, Jace, it turns out that he is a consultant to the FBI. He is there to protect the devices we are investigating, and he is also supposed to watch over us at work. Sorry this is happening Ade. When are you planning on leaving?" "I will call my mom right now and make arrangements to go there tonight. It is a good thing I work remotely."

Jace picked up Annie at 6:00. "Right on time sir," said Annie. "You look nice Annie." "Jace, how come you didn't tell me you consult with the FBI, is there anything else you are not telling me? I am not comfortable with you keeping secrets from me. I know we just started seeing each other, but we have kind of made a connection. No more secrets, OK." Annie punched Jace gently in his right shoulder. Jace laughed and said, "Got it, mam" and he leaned over and gave Annie a light kiss. Annie grinned real big and said, "Ok, I am ready for Mexican food and green Chile now."

15

The next day at work was definitely different for everyone. Instead of being excited about the success they were having testing the devices, their thoughts were on their own physical safety. They all jumped every time someone passed by their lab. Josh was relieved that Ade and the kids had made it safe to her mom's home in Roswell. Dr. Hudson said he had alerted the local police there as well as the local FBI field office.

It was Jace that made an effort to calm everyone's nerves. "I know things are weird, but I have got your back. We have people at the entrances and in the halls looking out for any potential problems. I am also carrying my weapon today in case a situation escalates within the building." Annie immediately said, "Jace, do you really think that it could that bad? We are just testing devices and running some crazy analysis." Josh laughed, which helped break the tension, "Annie, are you implying that my test technique is crazy?" Everyone laughed and Annie immediately said, "Woops, wrong word, I meant this incredible and powerful test technique." "Thanks Annie," Josh said grinning. "Ok guys, let's get started."

Right then Jordan walked into the lab, scaring everyone. "Just checking on the status of the devices from France, why are you guys just standing around?" "Jordan, it is not your place to come into my lab and tell my staff what to do, enough is enough. You are welcome to leave right now" said Josh angrily. "In fact, you are not welcome in here anymore. Go see Dr. Rico if you have questions, thank you."

With that said, Josh turned back to the test jigs. Jordan made some grumbling noise and left the lab. Annie, was the first to speak up, "Way to go Dr. B., that should shut him up." Jace said, "Nicely done Dr. Baker." "We'll see how long he stays away," said Josh

"Annie, I got an idea for modifying the test procedure. Remember that spike we saw on the transient when we were doing a pulse response test of the South Korean devices. That might be something we can focus on, it is definitely a unique feature," said Josh. "And we saw that with devices with altered architecture." "Good idea, Josh," said Annie. "Ok, let's call up the pulse test for the device from France. This is the device we were using for the deep learning. Unfortunately, we couldn't get the training number down to a low enough number. Let's call up the file and look at the pulse test." Annie entered some keystrokes, and the file was displayed on the scope. "See, look right there right after the pulse reaches a maximum point. Annie, Jace, is there a way we can just limit the range so that the neural network will just train on that range?" "Sure, said Jace, I should be able to do that without any problem." Annie and Jace worked on getting everything setup. When they were done, they said, "ready to go Dr. B." "Josh said, "Go ahead and start the deep learning of the neural network. We should be able to review the results maybe late tomorrow or Thursday. I am going to walk over to Dr. Rico's office, I will be back soon."

Josh walked to Dr. Rico's office. He noticed that he was super aware of the surroundings, "I guess I am a little nervous about things," Josh said to himself. As Josh almost got to Dr. Rico's door, the door opened, and Jordan and Daniel seemed to be having a serious discussion. Josh said. "Sorry to bother you but I just wanted to update you on the pulse tests." "Please go-ahead Josh," said Daniel. Jordan stayed standing by Daniel. "We are now testing the devices from the U.S. The neural network is being trained and we are planning to get results maybe tomorrow." "What about the devices from France," asked Jordan. "The results for those devices should be ready by Thursday. We are having a lot of difficulties, but we think we have a possible solution. We hope to know something by Thursday or sooner." "The funding agency for this work will want a better answer than that," said Jordan. Daniel spoke up and said, "Jordan, take it easy, let's deal with that some other time, we all have many other things on our minds right now." Keeping with tradition, Jordan just grumbled some words and started walking off. "Josh, how are you handling this and your family, are they okay, asked Daniel? "Just a little nervous and lonely, the family have all gone to Roswell to stay with Ade's mom until this situation gets resolved. Thanks for asking," said Josh. "You bet and let me know if there is anything I can do to help you. Are you up for lunch today, I think I hear Los Campos calling," said Daniel. "Sounds great," said Josh. "I will ask Annie and Jace to join us, their nerves are a little on edge too," said Josh. "I will meet you guys in the lobby at 11:30, see you then," said Daniel.

Josh got back to the lab and said, "We are joining Dr. Rico for lunch today at Los Campos, hope that is okay for you guys." "That sounds great Dr. Baker," said Jace. "I love the chicken flautas and guacamole." Annie spoke up and said, "I have never eaten there, but that sounds good to me too." "We are meeting Dr. Baker downstairs at 11:30," said Josh. In the meantime, have any additional devices for testing been delivered." "Nothing new today, as of yet," said Annie. "We have devices from France being prepared for evaluation, in fact, we now have two different neural networks being trained. The U.S. devices are here, and we have started the training process for those devices. We should have results for both groups sometime tomorrow afternoon or Thursday." "Thanks for the update Annie, you guys are making good progress," Josh said as he glanced at his watch. "Time to go to lunch, I am hungry.

They met Daniel in the lobby, and they all got into Josh's Honda CRV. The restaurant was already busy, and the smell of Mexican food filled the air. They all sat down at a table and ordered their food. Jace got the Chicken flautas, Josh and Daniel both got the green enchiladas. Annie took the longest to place her order. She finally settled on the combination plate. "I think I am hungry," said Annie with a smile.

Daniel said, "Thanks for joining me for lunch today. I just wanted to say that you are all doing a good job. We are all very anxious to see your results from testing the devices. This is new territory for the group. I just wanted to say that the funding agency is not concerned, I am not sure where Jordan is coming up with these things, everyday he keeps saying that the funding is in jeopardy. I have not heard any of these comments from any of those money people. Can you go ahead and give me an update since we are all together?

Josh was the first to speak, "Things are going well but the devices from France have been somewhat of a challenge. Our first attempt with training the neural network did not go well. However, Jace and Annie have made some adjustments to the test procedure that look promising." Annie spoke up and said with a little pride in her voice, "We happened to notice that the waveform for the pulse response had a unique artifact resting on the waveform." Jace jumped in and said, "Yes, we have modified the data so that the neural network will focus on that specific feature when it is training." Annie excitedly added. "This time we are confident that the neural network will train down to a score of 0.03 or less."

"Have you been able to detect any devices with altered architecture," asked Daniel? Josh quickly answered, "We received some devices from South Korea that had both good devices and some with altered architecture. We were told which devices were good and which were altered and, in that case, we trained the neural network using one good device and using one altered architecture device. When the training was complete, and we blindly tested all of the devices and we had about a 75% success rate of detecting altered devices. We didn't catch all the altered devices but it was better than a coin toss. Fortunately, having examples of both 'good' and 'altered' devices helped us to get the results we were looking for." "How about the devices from France, are there both good and altered architecture

Jeff Beasley

devices," asked Daniel? "We don't know," said Annie. We expect to have results tomorrow or Thursday." "This is exciting," said Daniel. "I tell you what, lunch is on me today." Everyone said thanks and then they got up and headed back to ESL.

After arriving back at ESL, Josh and Annie cleaned up the packing material from the devices from the U.S. fab. Jace played around with the current probes. They talked about their day and were relieved that things appeared somewhat normal. Then Jace and Annie set up a test using both a good device and an altered South Korean device. They then set up a circuit that took the pulsed current from the current probe and actually amplified the signal. The amplified output was played over a speaker in the lab. Jace put a good device in the test jig and put the playback of the pulse into a repeat mode. The signal coming over the speaker sounded like a bee buzzing. Jace and Annie looked at each other and both said, "Way cool!" They then put an altered architecture device in the test jig. They repeated the procedure with the repeating pulse test and then listened to the buzzing. Jace said, "Hey Annie, do you notice the difference in the buzzing sounds. I clearly hear two distinct buzzing sounds." Annie enthusiastically said, "I hear the difference too." They both got quiet, looked at each other and Jace said, "Hey Dr. Baker, you need to listen to this!"

Josh came over and said, "What's up"? Annie and Jace excitedly showed Josh what they had set up. "Do you want to hear the audio," said Jace. "Of course," replied Josh. Annie pushed enter on the keyboard and they listened to the audio playback for the pulse test of the 'good' device. Annie then selected the audio playback for the pulse test of the device with the altered architecture. Josh listened very carefully and asked Annie to set things up so Josh could do an A/B comparison. "Guys, this is excellent, I can actually hear the difference in the two sounds. I did this kind of audio analysis a few years back when I was searching for a way to detect defects or using this as a way to provide early detection for devices that were headed

60

for failure. This is really good. Can you repeat this for all of the devices in the South Korean lot?"

Jace and Annie both said, "Of course, we already have the pulse response test files stored on the hard drive. They then began playing back the many pulse response tests through the speaker. Jace and Annie had to laugh. "This is so, not an analytical method for test and evaluation. Maybe we should have taken ear training classes instead of all the mathematics and engineering analysis classes," said Jace. Annie said, "Yes, but then we wouldn't have been so miserable in class." "Isn't that the truth, but the rewards …." Jace said.

As they listened to the multitudes of buzzing tunes from the playback of the pulse response, Annie said, It's incredible, I can actually tell the differences in the buzzing." Jace said, "OK, let's give it a try, is this a good or altered device?" "No, I can identify that there is a difference, but I can't tell which is the sound from a good or altered device, dude." Josh walked up and said, "What are you guys doing?" We are listening to the latest in alternative rock Dr. B. We have both good and alternative rock versions," said Jace smiling, "catchy isn't it." "If Ade was here, we would be dancing for sure.

Dr. Rico and Jordan walked into the lab and Dr. Rico said, "What's going on… we heard this strange buzzing noise and laughter. Are you guys having a party?" "No Daniel, we are just having fun with the pulse response data from the South Korea devices. We can actually tell the difference between good devices and altered devices just by listening to the audio playback. We are not sure what we can do with this information but …. It's just another tool for detecting altered devices … we think." "Plus, it sounds pretty cool," said Annie. "Just listen to this."

Annie played the looped pulse response signal for a good device. Now listen to this one." This time the buzzing sound was for an altered device. "Can you guys tell that there is a difference?" Dr. Rico gave a quizzical look and said, "Are you telling me that we are listening to devices you are pulsing?" "Yes," said Annie and Jace together. Jace added, "Annie has the pulse response for each device stored on her computer, she is just calling up different pulse sounds, and she has it playing in a looped mode. Pretty cool isn't it." "This is very interesting, will this technique work for all devices, like the devices from the U.S. or France," asked Dr. Rico? Josh immediately said, "The only thing we know for sure is that this technique works on the devices from South Korea. By tomorrow, we should know if our techniques work for all of the devices."

Dr. Rico and Jordan both looked at Josh and the test bench and said, "Wow, this is incredible." Jordan added, "This will definitely make the funding agency happy, excellent work Dr. Baker." "Yes. I agree with Jordan, this is excellent work," said Dr. Rico. Your funding agency will definitely be pleased but, I am not sure about the people making the devices with altered architecture. Where are you with the devices from France?" Josh proudly replied, "We are still completing the training phase for the neural networks." Annie excitedly spoke up, "We are expecting to have the neural nets trained by tomorrow and we hope to have results soon after." "This is excellent," said Dr. Rico, "We are very happy and thanks for taking time to demonstrate this to us." "Yes," said Jordan. "This is amazing." Dr. Rico checked his watch and pulled out a 3x5 note card and said, "we have another meeting, we will check back with you tomorrow afternoon, thanks again for your time" and they walked out of the lab.

After Dr. Rico and Jordan left, Josh said, "Hey guys, that went very well, thanks to both of you for your hard work, good job!" Annie said, "Thanks, Dr.Baker, hopefully tomorrow will be just as rewarding. Jace, you have been very quiet, what's up?" Jace replied, "There is something about Jordan that really bothers me, did you see the way he was checking out the devices, our test gear and did you see how he looked at the computers. It just doesn't seem right, my FBI training taught me to always be looking out for behaviors that don't fit the situation, and guys, this is one of those times. Obviously, he wasn't doing anything wrong that we know of but …". Josh spoke up, "Yea, I get what you are saying, Let's just stay focused on doing excellent work, and thanks again to both of you for your help."

As they closed up for the day, Josh said, "Guys, have a good evening and thanks again for the work. We have a couple of neural networks being trained; we now have a clever way to audibly detect altered devices. It has been s good day. I will see you both tomorrow." "Thanks," said Annie, "see you tomorrow." Jace simply said, "Tomorrow" as he turned to Annie. "Would you like to have a beer and some 'Bats?" Annie replied, "Sure, pick me up at 6:30 okay." "Sounds good, see you then," as he gave Annie a kiss on her cheek.

That evening, the text message on Etienne's burner phone said, *We have a problem. They have figured out a way to detect our devices.*

The text reply simply said, *Deal with it!*

16

Jace and Annie were enjoying their beer and 'Bats' at The Venue. "What a strange day," said Annie. "I hope that it starts feeling a little bit more like normal soon, all the other people here in the restaurant have no idea what we are dealing with. I guess that old saying 'ignorance is bliss' is true." Jace spoke up, "My colleagues at the FBI deal with this type of stress daily, I am not sure how they deal with it, but they learn to cope. I am lucky that I am just a consultant." Right then Annie and Jace heard the sirens for what appeared to be multiple fire trucks. "That doesn't sound good, it sounds like it is right down the street" said Jace. Right then multiple police sirens blasted. "Wow, said Annie. Let's go outside and see what's going on." Many of the customers left their food and drinks and went outside to see what was happening. Annie and Jace looked down the street and saw that the building where they worked had flames coming out of several windows. "Oh my goodness," said Annie. "What should we do Jace?" Jace just stared at the flames and said, "Let's walk down a little closer. There is nothing we can do but …. I don't know. Maybe we can find out what happened.

Annie and Jace walked the two blocks to ESL's burning building. "Oh crap," said Jace. "The flames are coming out of our lab window." Just then, Josh walked up. "Hey guys, this ….is ….not …..good." Josh just stared at the fire and the firefighters working hard to extinguish the flames. There were now three fire trucks and numerous police and emergency vehicles parked around the building. Numerous people were also now standing a safe distance from the building. "Josh were you still at work", asked Annie? "No," said Josh, "The supervisor for building security is the one who alerted me. He called me to make sure that none of us were still in the lab. Man, this is not good. This probably means that all of our devices and our test results have been destroyed, thank goodness that none of you were hurt. I just hope we have not lost everything." "Dr. Baker," said Annie. "I downloaded all of the pulse test files for the devices from South Korea and I was also able to download the pulse test files for the devices from France. I have them in my pocket on a flash drive." Jace laughed, "I did the same thing, I guess it is a good thing that that we listened to you about saving our work." Josh then said, "Thanks guys …, that is a relief. At least not having the devices will not slow down our current work. Hey look, they have put out the fire but I am sure everything was destroyed. We didn't have any flammable materials in the lab that I remember, I wonder what started the fire. Maybe they will tell us tomorrow. They all stared at the building all wondering what this means for the project and their jobs. "I am going back home now, You guys stay safe." "Thanks Dr. B., we will see you back at work in the morning" and Jace and Annie started walking back to the restaurant, holding hands.

"Jace," said Annie, "do you think that someone started the fire, they were saying that there have been text message exchanges between someone from France and our building concerning the devices we are testing." Jace said, "That is what I am thinking, it is too much of a coincidence." "Do your friends at the FBI have additional intel that they haven't shared yet," asked Annie. "I am not aware of anything else, but this fire has to raise numerous red flags for all of the agencies with offices in the building," said Jace. They were almost at The Venue and Annie said to Jace, "Can I stay with you tonight, I am a little nervous about all of this." Jace gave Annie a hug and said, "Of course, I can sleep on the couch so you can have your own space." Annie gave Jace a sheepish smile and said, "We'll see." They gave each other hugs and walked into the restaurant.

Jace said, "I think that there are beer and 'Bats' with my name on it waiting for me." "Hey, don't be selfish, some of it is for me too Mr. FBI Consultant," said Annie. "Of course, madam, I shall not be so selfish, my lady," said Jace. Annie just punched Jace in the shoulder and smiled real big.

The next morning, Josh, Annie, and Jace were allowed to go into the lab space after the forensics team had completed gathering all relevant evidence. They were met at the door by Dr. Rico. He told the group, "The initial findings indicate that the fire was intentional, the fire investigators found evidence of an accelerant, but the video cameras captured nothing, no one was seen entering or exiting the lab after you three closed up at 5:00." They entered the lab and saw that everything was totally destroyed. The test gear was melted and all that was left of their computers was melted plastic. The devices they were testing had all been placed in a safe before they left for the evening but all devices had been destroyed because of the intense heat.

They all looked at the destroyed lab and Josh said, "Daniel, what do we do now? All of our devices have been destroyed, the test gear is destroyed, and all of our pulse test results on those computers have been totally destroyed. Just then, Jordan walked into the lab, "Oh my ... this is worse than I had imagined. This is not going to make the funding agency happy, did you guys leave a soldering iron on when you left for the evening? I guess you are going to have to start your work all over, get new devices and run new tests if the funding agency allows it."

Josh looked at both Daniel and Jordan and said, "Well, the good news is that Annie and Jace, all made copies of the test files. They have not been analyzed yet but fortunately we still have the test results. Daniel quickly spoke up and said, "You have test data for the devices from France? That is fantastic." "Yes, and the test results for the devices from South Korea and some files for the U.S. devices." "Wow, aren't you lucky, where is the test data?" Asked Daniel. Annie proudly answered the question, "Jace and I both have a flash drive with the files stored on them." Daniel then said, "Do you want me to store the flash drives for you in my office?" Josh immediately replied, "Thank you, but I think I would prefer to let them hang onto the devices for now, we have spent a lot of time gathering that test data, I just feel more comfortable having the flash drives close by." "Same for us." Said Annie and Jace. Jordan spoke up and said, "You guys might want to rethink that, what happens if you lose the flash drives too? You don't have a good track record." "Thanks for your concern but we'll just keep the flash drives on us." Josh added, "I will make a copy of the files for myself too. That will give us three sets of the pulse tests." "Let me know if you change your mind," said Daniel, "My office is a safe location and you are welcome to use it for safekeeping." "Thanks Daniel for the offer, so what happens now" asked Josh. "The lab will be closed off until Monday." Said Daniel. "Consider the rest of the week to be vacation time. Just make sure that you let us know where you are in case the investigators have any questions." Annie and Jace quickly said, "We will be staying at my apartment, you have my contact information." "I will probably drive to Roswell tonight," said Josh. "My wife and kids and our dogs are staying with Ade's mom besides, it is the UFO Festival this weekend in Roswell. It should be a nice break."

Daniel and Jordan took some more time to survey the damage to the lab. Fortunately, the only other damage to ESL was from the smoke and some water damage. "This is quite a mess," said Daniel. "This is quite a problem for us and our clients." "I hope our funding source doesn't decide to select a different manager," said Jordan. "Same here," said Daniel. "It may take a little time to clean things up but we can do it, I am confident of that. I will talk with Gus from building security to see if they can assist with any potential clean up problems." "Good idea," said Jordan and tell them it needs to be quick."

17

Jace and Annie spent the rest of the day exploring the historic village of Mesilla adjacent to the Rio Grande River. "Let's go into the Fountain Theater and watch a classic movie, said Annie. "And eat some popcorn too!" Said Jace. They bought popcorn and proceeded to watch Casablanca. After the movie was over, they headed to La Posta to eat Mexican food. "Thanks, Jace," said Annie "this has been a nice break, how about some sopapillas too." They finished their La Posta combination plates and then they both ordered sopapillas, putting a heavy covering of honey on each and laughing as their hands became covered with sticky honey. "It's messy but it sure is good. This has been a lot of fun Annie and good food too, and I really like the company. Maybe we could go on a date sometime," said Josh. "I think we are beyond that point Jace," Annie said with a smile. Jace said, "Yes, we passed that point last night, are you ready to head back to your place?' "Maybe yours," said Annie. Both had smiles on as they headed to their car.

"Jace, isn't that one of the building security guys for ESL. Is he following us?" Asked Annie. Jace looked over Annie's shoulder, "Yea, that is Gus, he is probably just looking around like us. This situation with the text messages has made you a little paranoid Annie. Annie didn't say anything but looked at the building security guy. "Jace, let's walk around the corner and see if he follows us," said Annie. Jace and Annie quickly walked around the corner to the next street. There was no sign of the security guy anywhere. Annie said, "Yes, maybe I am just a little nervous. Hey, let's pick up some green Chile on the way home. I need some Chile pods for making enchiladas and rellenos." They walked to their car and drove down the street to the vendor with Chile pods hanging outside the entrance. Annie walked up to the vendor and said, "I need some medium and hot green Chile please. Annie paid the vendor, Jace put the Chile into their car and both of them got into the car. "That hot Chile is very hot, my eyes are already burning. I just love the smell of fresh green Chile." said Jace. "Me too," said Annie. "and wait till we roast the Chile later. Oh, we do have beer at the apartment right, you can't roast Chile without ceveza." "That's my girl and yes we do," said Jace. "Girl, where have you been all my life?" Asked Jace. "Pretty much with my face in textbooks, computer screens, or working in the lab. You are very surprising too, Jace, where have you been?" Asked Annie. "Unfortunately I was in a bad relationship, but not anymore," Annie laughed and gently punched Jace in the shoulder.

As they approached Annie's apartment Jace said, "someone is parked outside your place. Do you recognize the car?" "No, it doesn't look familiar, oh someone is getting out, that's the guy from building security." "They must have an update on the fire at work, Annie said. Jace and Annie got out of the car, each carrying a bag of green Chile peppers. Jace walked up to the ESL building security guy and said, "Hello Gus, what's up?" Gus pulled a gun from his jacket and said, "Let's go inside, now." "Gus, what the heck, what is this about?" "I said, inside now, no funny stuff," Jace and Annie slowly walked to the door of the apartment. Annie unlocked the door and they walked inside. Gus said, "Sit on the couch, both of you and don't do anything stupid."

"Gus, what is this about man?" Asked Jace. "You both have something I need, I think you know what it is!" Said Gus. Annie spoke up and said, "We have no idea what you are talking about, what is going on, WHAT DO YOU WANT!" Yelled Annie. Gus slapped Annie across her face, "Girl you know what I want! Where are the flash drives you used to store the pulse tests? "Seriously!" Said

Jace. Gus pushed his gun into Jaces's face and said, "Don't get stupid, Mr. FBI consultant, give me the flash drives, both of you, now!"

Jace started to reach into his pants and Gus yelled, "Nothing stupid, understand...." Jace slowly reached into the pockets of his pants and pulled out a red flash drive. "Slowly, ... I said slowly ... hand it to me." Gus still had the gun pointed towards Jace and Annie. Gus put the flash drive into his pants pocket and said, "Ok missy, now yours. Annie looked at Jace, she had total fear on her face and then slowly inserted her hand into her purse. Annie said, "I can't find it, I need to dump out my purse to get it. Gus said, 'Don't do anything stupid." Annie pulled her purse off her shoulder and tightly holding the purse straps, Annie let out a loud screech, swung her purse violently around her neck and over her head and slamming it into Gus's head.

The totally surprised assailant let out a loud moan and reached for his head with both hands. Jace saw the opportunity and he grabbed the hand holding the gun and yanked Gus's arm, twisting it hard behind Gus's back. The gun fell to the ground and Gus violently swung at Jace's head making a full connection. The hit caused Jace to fall to the ground, knocking the gun close to Annie. Gus saw the opportunity to grab the gun and started reaching for it. Annie saw Gus coming closer to her and for the gun. She looked for something she could use to protect herself. The bag of 'hot green Chile' peppers were in the chair beside her. A broken hot green Chile pod was at the top of the sack, Annie reached for it just as Gus reached for the gun, Annie shoved the broken hot Chile pepper pod into Gus's eyes. The juices from the hot green pepper sprayed on his eyes and his face and the hot Chile immediately began burning his eyes and face. Gus put his hands on face and screamed, "You bitch!!, oh god, oh god, oh god. Jace rolled over and grabbed the gun and pointed it at Gus and he yelled out, "Down on the ground, down on the ground and put your hands behind your back. Gus did as he was told and while still moaning from the burning sensation created by the hot Chile, Jace took his belt off and used it to secure Gus's hands and sat on his back.

Annie picked up her cell phone and called 911. Annie screamed into the phone that a man attacked them and Jace had the guy secured. They told Annie that officers were on the way. While Jace was still sitting on Gus's back, Annie ran into her kitchen and pulled out several zip ties. She rushed to where Jace was sitting, handed him the zip ties and Jace secured Gus's hands and his feet. Jace stood up, almost falling over. "Annie, are you okay, did he hurt you when he slapped you." "No, I am okay, I bet your head hurts though, are you okay?" Said Annie. They both hugged each other, "This is crazy, are you sure you are ok. Jace". "Yes, I will be okay."

Right then two police cars pulled into the apartment complex. Jace met the officers at the door and showed the officers his badge. Jace told the officers he and Annie had secured the assailant. The officers told Jace to sit down and they asked where the woman was that placed the 911 call. Jace said, "She is right inside the door, and she is okay." An ambulance then pulled up.

The EMT's quickly assessed the situation and began treating both Annie and Jace for their injuries. Annie's right cheek was bright red, but she didn't sustain any other injuries. The EMT's checked where Jace was struck and they performed multiple tests and determined that other than a sore spot on his head, he was going to be fine.

The police pulled Gus up and read him his rights. Gus yelled out, "There are more of us coming, you better watch out!" The police officers then quickly escorted Gus to the police car and placed him in the back seat. One officer returned and said, "Do I need to call anyone for you guys, are you okay." Jace said, "I am okay, Annie how about you?" Annie replied, "I am okay, just still shaking like crazy. What did Gus mean that there are 'more coming'?" "I have no idea," said Jace.

A detective then showed up at Annie's apartment and asked Jace and Annie to sit down with him. The detective asked, "Why do you think the guy attacked you?" Jace said, "I honestly have no idea, I know that he is part of the building security where we both work." "Where do you both work?" Asked the detective. "We are both engineers and we work in the ESL building, on the university campus" said Annie. "Why do you think he was targeting you?" Asked the detective. "I am not sure; we just do analysis and testing of integrated circuits. The guy wanted the flash drives containing our test results." "Hey, was it your lab that caught on fire yesterday, we heard it was arson? Asked the detective. "Yes, it is where we work." "Have you seen this guy before?" Asked the detective. "Yes," said Annie, He is with building security at ESL, I have seen him many times in the building aligning cameras, and double checking doors, and the building perimeter, basic physical security stuff. But, other than that, I don't really know him."

"Who's is your boss at ESL," asked the detective. Annie replied, "Dr. Josh Baker and he answers to Dr. Rico." "Is this a secure project?" "No sir." "Can you tell me anything about what information is in the files of your flash drive?" "They are just copies of pulse tests for integrated circuits." "What is a pulse test?" "It is a technique that Dr. Baker developed that enables us to analyze devices that have problems such as defects," said Annie. "And we have now modified the test to detect devices with altered architecture." "What does altered architecture mean?" Jace replied, "Basically, those are integrated circuit devices that have modified so that they are doing more than what was intended. Like providing back doors or transmitting secure information like passwords out on the Internet or stealing banking info and things like that." "Thanks," said the detective," I will get back to you if I need anything else."

The police finished up and said they would come back if they had questions. Everyone was gone and Jace and Annie just looked at each other. "Let's go shower and go to bed," said Annie. Jace grabbed Annie's hand and they both walked inside the apartment.

18

Josh had called Ade and told her he was driving to Roswell. He explained to her about the fire and how he was excited to see her, the kids, and the dogs. And yes, excited to see his mother-in-law too. Josh had made this drive many times. He always enjoyed passing through White Sands National Monument, Ruidoso, and the Hondo Valley. Josh was also excited to be in Roswell for the UFO Festival. The parade is just a lot of fun and the whole town dresses up in Alien costumes. Yes, believe it or not, aliens crashed outside Roswell in 1947, at least that is what some say. Ade's Dad's relatives were living in Roswell at the time and they said, crazy things were happening around town at that time. Ade's mom, Jackie, always just laughed it off, she said her theory was that alcohol and too many lonely nights on ranches probably created the legend, that and the fact that a weather balloon crashed there. Post WWII America was a different time with the cold war and the constant threat of a communist takeover. Josh just laughed to himself and said, "If I do see an alien, I am going ask them for help with the pulse tests. Obviously, they must be advanced and already know the all the answers. Maybe they know where Jimmy Hoffa is, you never know …. ".

Josh finally was exiting the Hondo Valley and approaching the rolling hills west of Roswell. Josh decided to pull his car over and stretch his legs. Josh noticed that another car pulled over too, about a ¼ mile behind Josh. Josh just laughed, guess that guy had to pea too. Josh got back into his car and pulled back onto US70. The car behind him also pulled out. Josh didn't think much about it but considering the fire and the warning from the FBI, Josh decided to pull out his cell phone in case he needed to make a call. The cell phone screen was black and when Josh tapped the screen, the screen remained black. He fiddled with cellphone until he figured out, "I forgot to put the phone on charge last night , crap". Josh looked at the mile marker and thought to himself, "I still have about 80 miles to go, oh well, I'll charge my phone when I get to Grandma Jackie's house. The rest of the drive was uneventful, but the car remained behind him the rest of the way. "Interesting,' said Josh to himself.

Eventually, Josh arrived in the west part of Roswell on West 2nd and he turned on Sunset and headed to Ade's mom's house on Poe street. The kids would always start yelling, "We are going to Grandma's" and the dogs added to the hysteria by barking and whining, anxious for Grandmas' special back rub. Josh pulled up into the driveway and noticed the kids were playing in the front yard. "Daddy's, here," said his kids Sara and Sean. Sara ran to the door and yelled out, "Mom, Grandma, Daddy's here." Ade and Jackie came out and Ade immediately said, "Why didn't you call?" Josh held up his phone and said, "The battery is dead, woops." Ade just shook her head. Josh gave Ade a hug and hugged her mom too. The dogs both looked at Grandma begging for a special back rub. Grandma bent down and gave each special loving.

The kids took time to show their Dad all the neat things that Grandma had purchased at a garage sale. Yes, that is where Ade gets her passion for antiques and collectibles. Once they all updated each other, Ade said, "Let's go downtown for the UFO parade and exhibits." The kids enthusiastically said yes, and Josh gave a "Thumbs Up." "Grandma, do you want to go too?" Asked Josh. "No, I'll stay here with the dogs. I will keep them entertained,"

Josh unpacked his car, and he and Ade loaded up the kids. They waved goodbye to Grandma and off to the UFO festival they went. Their daughter Sara looked at them very intently and asked, "Grandpa was here in 1947, do you think he saw the aliens?" "It is possible sweetheart, we always asked him that question but, Grandpa just smiled and said emphatically, I am from France." This was always his little joke because of the 'Coneheads' from Saturday Night Live who obviously were aliens, and they would always say they were from France." Special memories as we drove downtown. As Josh drove down the street, he noticed that the same car that was behind him as he drove to Roswell was parked down the street. "What are the odds." Josh just shook his head.

The signs on Main Street said, "The Invasion Is Now!" Josh and Ade laughed at the sign and at the many people decked out in space outfits and alien costumes. They spent most of the afternoon visiting all of the many exhibits enjoying the excitement. They took time to visit the UFO museum and the many other UFO shops on Main Street.

Ade's mom made herself some tea and sat at the coffee table. Her feet were propped up on the spare chair. She had put the dogs in the backyard since she didn't have a dog door, but she made sure both dogs received special loving and a back rub and of course, water and a special treat. Her doorbell rang and she got up to answer the door. She didn't recognize the person and she said, "Can I help you?" "The visitor said, "Is Dr. Baker available?" Ade's mom said, "No, they left for the UFO festival, they should be back about 5:00." "I will wait for them," said the stranger. Ade's mom said, "You can wait for them in your car, I can give you some water." "No," the stranger pulled out a gun and said, "No thanks, I will stay in the house with you." The stranger pushed Ade's mom back into the house and he followed her into the house.

Josh and his family were having a great time at the UFO Festival. The kids had transformed themselves into scary Martians with teeth that only a ghoul would appreciate. Ade too, had joined into the celebration by transforming herself into a creature from a planet not yet discovered. Josh chose to only purchase a nice hat with the logo,

Roswell UFO Festival

"We are not alone"

Everyone was having a great time. Josh was so happy to be with his family. He reached over and gave Ade a hug. Ade just looked at Josh and said, "What's that for?". I don't think I've ever hugged a creature from another planet before, I was just curious what it was like." Ade smiled and shook her head and said, "you are just trying to seduce an alien aren't you Mr. B?" "Maybe," replied Josh. Ade looked at her watch and said, "Hey kids, get everything together and let's head back to the car." The kids let out alien screeches, swinging the plastic alien sabers that they purchased at an exhibit. As they walked away, they grabbed Ade's and Josh's hands and off they went walking to their car. Sara was carrying a special bag for Grandma, she said it was Grandma's alien survival kit. Ade smiled as she looked inside the bag and saw the bag full of chocolate covered caramels with nuts. Ade thought, chocolate covered caramels might be good for me too. This has been a good day and I need a healthy snack. Ade just smiled.

There was a fair amount of traffic at the UFO Festival so it took them a little longer to get to Grandma's house. Josh noticed the car again down the street and he just shook his head. They all got out of the car as if they were invading an alien planet, swinging the sabers playfully yelling out, Grandma, we are home. Ade walked into Grandma's house first with the kids in tow. Josh followed closely. As soon as Josh got in the door, he sensed that something wasn't right, it was too quiet. They walked into the kitchen and Ade let out a scream, Jackie's hands were tied, and a stranger was standing by the sofa holding a gun. Josh yelled at the guy, "WHAT IS GOING ON?".

The kids then saw Grandma tied up and both Sara and Sean screamed. Sara began to shiver and cry, Ade reached for her daughter trying to comfort her and yelled out, "ARE YOU OKAY MOM?".

The dogs on the back porch began to howl and dance nervously round the back door. Sean immediately grabbed Josh's hand. Josh glared at the stranger and said, "WHAT ARE YOU DOING?" The room was now in total chaos with the kids crying, the dogs barking, Ade trying to help her mom and Josh yelling at the stranger.

The stranger screamed out, "EVERYONE SHUT UP NOW!!" This just made the dogs bark more and scared the kids. The stranger looked at Josh and yelled, "GIVE ME THE FLASH DRIVE NOW!!" Josh looked at the guy and yelled, "WHAT ARE YOU TALKING ABOUT!!" This just made the dogs even more agitated and increased the rate of their dancing on the back porch. The stranger yelled back, "THE ONE WITH THE PULSE TESTS, NO MORE MESSING WITH ME." as he abruptly grabbed Josh's daughter and pointed the gun at her. The stranger yelled, "I DON'T WANT TO HURT HER, JUST GIVE ME THE FLASH DRIVE, NOW!. The dogs were now violently agitated, barking and scraping at the back door. Josh looked at the stranger and reached into his pants pocket and pulled out the flash drive. The stranger reached his hand out for the drive when suddenly there was an enormous crashing sound at the back door. Moco, their German shepherd had just busted down the back screen door and was coming directly for the stranger. The dog jumped at the guy and bit hard on the hand that held the gun. The stranger dropped the gun and tried wrestling with Moco. This didn't slow down the angry dog, she just found more places to bite. Moco then bit the stranger between the legs. The scream could have been heard for miles. The stranger ran for the front door, holding his crotch, bursting through the door only to find Josh and Ade's Doberman Pincher, Tobi looking right at him. The stranger started to run when Tobi jumped at him and violently grabbed his leg. The stranger collapsed on the ground, crying out in pain now with both dogs sitting on his back.

Josh immediately grabbed their kids and Ade cut her mom's restraints while the dogs were still sitting on the stranger. Josh called 911 and the dogs were still sitting there when two police cars arrived.

Josh called his dogs off the back of the stranger and told the police what had happened. The police talked to Ade and her mom and made sure the kids were okay before taking the stranger to the police station. Ade looked at Josh and asked, "What in the world are you involved with?" Josh calmly replied, "The drive is just a copy of test data from work, I am not sure why they want it, we haven't verified anything yet." "Does this have anything to do with why you had me come to Roswell, … for my safety?" "Yes," said Josh, "I am so sorry Ade….. I am very sorry. Let's go check on the kids and Grandma," Ade said, "OK."

After a little time, Josh called the number the FBI staff member at ESL had provided him. "Dr. Hudson, this is Josh Baker, I need to make you aware of a situation in Roswell." Josh explained what had happened and Dr. Hudson said, "I will have Special Agents on site in 20 minutes.

19

On Sunday, after a lot of debate, Ade decided to go back home with Josh and the kids. The drive back was very quiet, definitely lacking the excitement that Josh felt driving up. "Josh," said Ade, "You put the kids, my mom, and me in danger. You can't do that again." "Ade, I know, I am very sorry, I didn't know that they would follow me or that they even knew where your mom lived. I promise not to put you and the kids in danger again." Ade just looked forward, her eyes focused on an empty space, as they made the quiet drive back home.

Josh showed up at work on Monday. He met Dr. Rico in the lobby as well as Jace and Annie. They both looked like they had involved in a wreck or something like that. They told Josh what had happened, and Josh told them of the experience he and his family had. Everyone was mortified that this happened. Dr. Rico said a new lab was ready for them, it would be a couple of months before the renovation of their old lab would be completed. Dr. Rico asked if each still had their flash drives. Each pulled out a device to show him. Dr. Hudson stopped by and asked them to join him in the conference room.

All of them gathered in the conference room. Dr. Hudson updated them on the police reports and what the detectives had uncovered. Gus, who attacked Annie and Jace admitted that he was working with some associate in France but only knew his first name. He said he didn't know where they worked or if they were working with another group. He said he was also aware of the burner phone and the text message exchanges. He had also arranged to have a guy follow Josh to Roswell. That guy didn't know anything else other than that his objective was to retrieve a flash drive. Both of the assailants were under arrest and faced years in jail. Dr. Rico asked, "Dr. Hudson, are you aware of anyone else involved with this?" Dr. Hudson replied, not at this time, but I will ask you three to be extra cautious and report anything suspicious. Annie, Jace, and Josh just looked at each other and mouthed, "Well crap." Dr. Hudson said, "Be very thorough with the testing of the devices from France. Since Gus had a connection with someone from France, my gut feeling is that there must be something special about those devices. Josh looked at Annie and Jace and just nodded his head.

ESL provided Josh with another lab with various pieces of test gear. They also got computers, monitors, oscilloscopes, and current probes. Annie began setting up the neural network software on the computers. Jace began to assemble the test jigs for the new devices they were expecting. Josh spent time on the phone with HR and the police concerning the fire in the lab. ESL had also requested that he fill out a loss report for all the equipment and computers that had been damaged. Fortunately, Josh had recent inventory reports to work from. It was taking quite some time for Josh to get all the inventor ID's for the destroyed devices. He just sighed and said to Annie and Jace, "After what happened this past weekend and the fire, it is hard to get my brain back to thinking about doing normal work. I imagine you guys feel that way too." Jace spoke out and said, "Yes, I can imagine the terror that you were dealing with, your poor wife, your kids and your mother-in-law and that crazy intruder. "Yes, it was horrible, how about you guys, how are you holding up?" Annie rubbed her cheek and said, "It hurst less every day, at least I can now smile without hurting. Mentally, I guess that it will take some time to heal." "Jace, how about you, how are you holding up?" Asked Josh. "I am okay, I was just scared for Annie." Annie reached over and gave Jace a quick hug. "Besides, she would beat me up if I let anything happen to her." Annie then punched Jace softly in the shoulder, "That's my girl" said Jace laughing, and Josh laughed too.

Everyone got back to work. Annie finally got the neural network software running on her computer and said, "Ok, I am going to start the deep learning for the data we collected on the devices from France. We should have results by tomorrow afternoon. I am also going to start another run with the neural networks where the training pattern will be focused on the artifacts we saw on the devices from France. Not sure what that will reveal but ... we might be able to see something interesting, we will just have to wait and see." Josh said, "Sounds good Annie ... Jace, how are you coming with the test jig?" "Everything is going well, we just need more devices to test, but the test jig will be ready soon."

Josh then said, "Let's repeat that situation where we just listened to the audio playback of the pulse test data. I guess I just want to hear that bussing sound again, maybe there is something in there we are missing." Jace said, "Let me get that set up. We have the pulse tests stored on the flash drives and we can just loop the audio. Just let me go get some speakers and the amplifier, I will be right back." Jace left for the supply room and Josh took the opportunity to ask Annie. "So, you two are a couple now, he sure speaks well of you and the way he looks at you." Annie smiled really big with both cheeks now turning bright red and said, "I don't know, It just happened. We seemed to connect in so many ways, I really like him. How did you and Ade meet up?" "Ade's dad is from France which is where I first met her. I spent six months over there working on a project. Right after I left, her dad took a job with an oil company and the family moved to Roswell where they already had family living there. That is where we started seeing each other. I was working in Las Cruces, going to graduate school, and I would make the drive up to Roswell two or three times a month. Ade later came to the university and we have been together ever since. I told her that the first time I saw her that she was going to be my girl. My friends all said I was crazy but .... It came true, miracles do happen. Now, 10 years later, two kids, a new job, and crazy things happening to all of us. Life is funny." "It is crazy," said Annie. "I never expected to meet someone and Jace was so grumpy when he started working with us. Come to find out he was having relationship problems, but lucky for me we connected. I think he may be the one but don't tell him that." Annie had that big smile on her face again. "We just had two of the worst days and I was just glad that he was there with me." "I bet he is glad that you bought hot green Chile too." "Yes, that was fortunate for us but not for Gus, he probably prefers red Chile." Annie said laughing." Thanks for sharing Dr. Baker." "My pleasure and thank you too."

Jace returned from the supply room with the speakers and an audio amplifier. Jace and Annie grinned at each other when he came in the room. Josh noticed them looking at each other and said, "Geez guys, you have only been apart for 15 minutes. Do I need to leave?" Annie giggled and said, "Jace, Dr. Baker knows about us. He figured it out." Jace immediately said, "Dr. Baker, I hope that doesn't cause a problem. We promise to be professional." Josh just laughed and said, "No problems guys, I am very happy for you."

They set things up and began listening to the looped pulse test audio. They all smiled at the buzzing sounds coming from the playback. Jace said, "Did you hear that, it sounds like a lower frequency sound, it is very brief, but it is different than the repetitive buzzing sound. Annie pulled out the paperwork on the devices, double checked the file that was playing and smiled. "Hey Dr. Baker, the device we are listening too is one with altered architecture." Josh smiled and said, "Maybe we are on the right track. Annie, let's hope the neural networks do their magic tomorrow. "I am confident it is going to work," said Annie. Jace and Annie began going through all the pulse tests for the devices from South Korea and they were pleased that they could hear subtle differences.

Jordan came into the lab and said very loudly. "Your buzzing noise can be a little annoying and I can hear it quite well now that your lab is now in the same wing as my office. Is it really necessary to make the noise, can you wear headphones or turn it down?" Jordan continued to quiz the group, "Are you having any success, have you found the devices that were supposedly shipped from Europe that have modified architecture?" Josh replied and said, "The devices we are working with are from South Korea and yes some have altered architecture. We have not retested the devices from France yet, the neural net is still being trained. We hope to test those devices on Wednesday." "So, are you having any success with the devices from South Korea?" asked Jordan. Jace spoke up and said, "Interestingly enough, we can hear a difference with the pulse tests. We made some changes to the pulse waveform, and we do notice a slight difference. As Dr. Baker said, "We hope to verify this with the neural net tomorrow." Jordan just looked at the three and said, "Well at least maybe you can keep the noise down in the meantime." With the said, Jordan walked out of the lab.

As Jordan walked out, Dr. Rico walked in. "Hey everyone, just checking on how things are going. Dr. Hudson mentioned the devices from France, how is that going?" Josh replied, "We started retraining the neural networks today. It is a deep learning, so we don't expect results for a day or two. We are getting some interesting results for the devices from South Korea though. Annie, Jace, please demonstrate the audio tests for Dr. Rico." Annie said, "Glad to help, the first sound you will here is from a known good device." Annie started the playback and then said, "Okay, this is the sound for an altered device. Did you hear the difference?" Dr. Rico just grimaced and shook his head no. Annie said, "Okay, let's try it again, this is a good device. Now this is an altered architecture." She repeated alternating the sounds for another minute. Dr. Rico smiled and said, "I hear the difference, WOW, so what you are showing is that indeed there is a difference. Since there is a difference, what exactly does that mean?" Jace proudly spoke up and said, "Dr. Baker has told us that good devices will all generate a unique sound, devices that produce a different sound indicate the devices either has a defect or have been altered. The bottom line is that devices of certain type produce the same unique sound." Josh looked proudly at Jace and said, "What he said is exactly correct, we have proven we can identify altered devices, but we have not proven that when we don't have an altered devices to train on. We are optimistic but won't have results for a least two days." Dr. Rico said, "This is fantastic everyone. You have all done an amazing job. Thanks for sharing with me." Dr. Rico shook everyone's hands said, "Good job!" And he left.

That evening, there was a text message on Etienne's burner phone, *It looks they have figured out how to detect our devices.*

The text message on the burner phone at ESL displayed *I am catching a flight tonight. They have to be stopped!*

20

Without a doubt, Josh, Annie, and Jace were on cloud nine after hearing Dr. Rico's praise of their accomplishments. Josh was beaming, having a hard time not letting out a big yell. But the rational side of himself just said, "Ok, let's get back to work." They pulled the pulse response tests files for the devices from France. They then began playing the sounds of the repeated pulses. They were being extra careful, just listening for any difference. They completed listening to the sounds from all 30 devices. They didn't hear any differences, no special 'unique' sound. Josh said, "Let's try it again, I don't want to have to wait for the neural network to be trained. But, if we don't hear any differences or unique sounds, it just might mean the devices are all good.

They listened carefully to the buzzing sound each device generated, and Annie said, "Let's play that one again and compare it to the first device. They played the sounds several times and then Annie said, "That's it, do you hear that low thud sound. Play it again Jace." They all listened carefully, Jace replayed the two sounds several more times and then both Josh and Jace said, "I hear a thud." That is very similar to the sound that the devices from South Korea exhibited. "Dr. Baker, does this mean the devices from France have altered architecture?" Asked Annie. "I think it does, let's listen to all the devices once again and keep a log of which devices have the bump sound. I am reluctant to say that we have identified anything until we have the confirmation from the neural network but in the meantime, "Great job, guys! Tomorrow we will hopefully have trained neural networks probably by mid-afternoon. Annie, Jace, let's go ahead and call it a day. *Son las cinco en otra lugar* [It's 5 o'clock somewhere]. "Gracias, Jefe" said Jace. "Gracias doctor Baker," said Annie. Annie and Jace just smiled at each other and left the building holding hands. Josh called Ade and told her he was headed home.

The plane from Dallas via Paris, arrived in El Paso at 7:35PM. A foreboding man from France stepped off the plane into the El Paso International Airport terminal. He picked up his luggage, went outside and waited for his Lyft to Las Cruces. Once he was on his way, he used the burner phone and called his contact at ESL. He said, "I am staying at an Airbnb tonight close to the ESL building. I will send you my contact information when I arrive. We will need to discuss our next steps then." He closed the phone and slept the rest of the way to Las Cruces.

Ade was excited to see Josh home early. She told him about the kids and their latest activities at school. Ade told Josh that tomorrow there was going to be a huge estate sale at the church, and she was planning to be there. She was very excited because the dealer's online site was advertising some of her favorite antiques. She said she had her eye on a really cool antique 'sad iron' with the original wooden handle. Josh gave Ade a big hug and said, "I hope you can get it; it sounds perfect." Ade said," Hopefully no one beats me to it, you know how I get when I lose." Josh said, "I would not want to get on your bad side either." Ade shook her head and hit Josh's shoulder and just smiled.

The next day Josh was greeted by Annie and Jace as he walked into the lab. Annie excitedly said, "The neural network has been trained down to our target of 0.03. Not sure how it completed training ahead of schedule but, we are ready to test all of the other devices." Jace loaded up the pulse test files and said, "Ok, here we go." The first device produced a result of 0.28. Everyone just smiled. The second device produced a score of .031. The next 15 devices produced similar scores. Josh just looked at Annie and Jace and said,

"I hope this doesn't mean that the neural network is not working. Let's try another one Jace." Jace set up the neural network for the next pulse test and a score of 0.891 was generated. Josh quickly said, "Run another test." Jace set up everything and a score of 0.892 was displayed. Try another device Jace. The next device produced a score of 0.99. The next 7 devices produced similar scores. Josh just looked at Annie and Jace and said, "We don't know if any of the devices from France have altered architecture for sure but based on the results we just obtained and the fact that the bad guys were trying to take our files, I am going to assume the devices have been altered. The good news, unless I am missing something, is we have just verified that our test technique can detect integrated circuits with an altered architecture. Good job guys!" They all hugged each other and then realized, "What now?" Josh came out of his shock and said, Annie, call Dr. Hudson from the FBI. Tell him it's crucial that he comes down right now.!"

Ade was having her usual fun at the estate sale at the church. The look on Ade's face was priceless when she spotted the 'sad iron' with the wooden handle. Ade picked it up and said to herself, "Ladies in the old days must have been very strong, this iron weighs several pounds." Right then a man bumped into Ade. She just looked at the foreboding man and said, "Excuse me sir, I will move in a minute." She gave the man a very dirty look. Ade paid for the items she had purchased and was still a little irritated with that man, who had just bumped right into her. She opened her car door and was putting her purchases on the seat when she felt strong hands on her neck. She tried to squirm away, but the hold was too strong. A gravelly voice said, "Get in the car, don't say anything and you won't get hurt." Ade got into the car and the man said, "where is your phone?" Ade pulled out her phone and the man said, "Call your husband, don't say anything stupid. I will tell him what I need, CALL HIM NOW!" Ade picked up her phone and dialed Josh.

Josh's phone buzzed and he picked it up and said, "What's up Ade?" A gravelly voice sternly said, I got your wife and you have something I need. If you want your wife back safely then I need all the devices from France destroyed and any test data you have collected destroyed. Do you understand!" Josh pushed the speaker button on his phone. "So, you are telling me that you have my wife and I must destroy all of the devices and data from the devices from France. I need to speak to my wife, NOW." Ade's scared voice came over the phone. Josh, please .. do … as … he … says." The gravelly voice said, "I have someone at ESL monitoring your situation and I will release your wife as soon as he confirms that you have followed my instructions, UNDERSTAND!." Josh said, "How do I know you aren't going to hurt my wife!" The man said, "QUIT STALLING, DO AS I SAID, I JUST TOLD YOU THAT I HAVE A MAN AT ESL. I WILL RELEASE YOUR WIFE WHEN I GET CONFIRMATION YOU HAVE DONE WHAT I REQUESTED!" With that Josh's speaker on his phone went quiet. A hand padded his back and said, "Good job, You kept him on the phone long enough for my guys to trace the call and establish his location!" Josh turned around and looked at Dr. Hudson and said thank you.

Ade was petrified of the man. He was very big and scary. Ade looked around trying to figure out a way to escape. The man kept checking his phone, obviously to see if he received confirmation that Josh had destroyed the devices from France and deleted any associated test data. Just then the sounds of sirens could be heard. The man started looking around everywhere for any police cars. Ade used this opportunity to grab the heavy metal 'sad iron' by its wooden handle and then she swung it very hard at the man's head. Her aim was dead on and the pointy end of the 'sad iron' connected perfectly with the man's forehead. The man screamed in agony from the sharp pain and from being hit on the head by a very heavy object. The pointy end made a large cut on the assailants' forehead and blood was pouring out of his head. Ade took the opportunity to jump out of the car with the man still screaming from the pain. Right then a city police car and an unmarked vehicle pulled up.

Ade dropped the 'sad iron' and ran to the officer screaming, HELP ME, THAT MAN ATTACKED ME. The other car had two FBI field agents and when they saw the bloodied man in the car, they immediately rushed to the car. The man was pulled out of the car, handcuffed, and read his rights. The FBI agents searched the man, and they found a gun and a phone. EMT's were called to take care of the man's bleeding head and the officer collected Ade's statement. She was shaking the whole time and rubbing her hands together uncontrollably.

It took Ade quite some time to recover from the attempted abduction. The police officer came over and said, "Are you okay ma'am." She shook her head yes that she was okay. The officer asked the EMT's to check her out. Fortunately, other than her nerves, Ade was fine. The FBI agents approached Ade and said, "Dr. Hudson at ESL has requested that we escort you to ESL. He wants you and your husband to see each other. Will that be okay?" Ade thanked the Agents, said "YES" and they all climbed into their cars and drove to ESL.

Dr. Hudson received confirmation that the man who attacked Ade had been arrested. Dr. Hudson said, "Dr. Baker, I need you to tell your staff and managers that due to an unfortunate accident, all materials related to the devices from France have been destroyed. Josh said, "Because of the fire, we only have computer files left." "Tell them that those files have unfortunately been destroyed too," said Dr. Hudson. "But why are we doing this? Has the man who attacked Ade been arrested?" Asked Josh. Dr Hudson said, "Yes, Ade is fine, I have asked the Agents on site to escort her here. As for getting the whole ordeal behind us, I have an idea." He looked at Josh and said with a smile, "We are going fishing. I will request everyone to meet in the conference room in just a few minutes so maybe we can wrap all of this up. Someone will be coming for you soon to escort you to the conference room."

Josh, Annie, and Jace went back to work in the lab. A little while later, Dr. Rico and Jordan Pines came to the door and said, "We have all been called to an emergency meeting in the conference room. You need to come now. Everyone stopped what they were doing and headed to the conference room. Dr. Sassenfeld, Dr. Hudson, several team managers, and the head of building security and some of the staff were present as well as two gentlemen they had never seen before. They all sat down and Dr. Hudson stood and said, "Thanks for coming down on short notice. As you all know, we have had a crazy week. We had a fire in Dr. Baker's lab, and Dr. Baker has just formed me that all the pulse response files from South Korea and France have been erased with no chance of recovery. Annie and Jace were attacked by someone trying to take their flash drive. Dr. Baker and his family were also attacked, and the guy wanted his flash drive too. This is both a serious and crazy situation. This has got to stop. Our intel tells us that the people from France are working with someone at ESL. I need to know, do any of you have any idea who at ESL might be behind this." There was dead silence in the conference room. Everyone was just looking at everyone else. Most just shrugged their shoulders. No one said anything and the silence was deafening …..

Right then a cell phone started ringing, startling everyone and everyone began looking around. The cell phone continued to ring, and Jordan stood up and he said, "Excuse me, but I have an important call I need to take" and he started to exit through the door. Jordan opened the door, and two police officers were waiting outside the door. Jordan said, "Excuse me, I need to get buy, please." Right then, Dr. Hudson and the two gentlemen who were in the conference room walked up behind Jordan and said, "Can I see your phone, Jordan?" Jordan said "No, it … is … not my phone, I am holding it for someone else." Dr. Hudson said, "Maybe we should go down to the police station and try to locate the owner." Jordan just glared at Dr. Hudson. "Hand me the phone Jordan. Jordan did nothing. "Just FYI," said Dr. Hudson, "the call you just got on your phone was placed by my Agents"

Jordan immediately spoke out, "That is absurd, this phone belongs to my …. Sister. She may need my help. I demand that you let me pass." Dr. Hudson then said, "Jordan, If you will check your phone you will see that your most recent call was from Etienne's burner phone, your contact in France and who we now have in custody. The look on Jordan's face was priceless. He new his little game was over. He just looked at Dr. Hudson and said, "Well, c'est la vie [That's life]. Dr. Hudson laughed, "In all honesty, we had no idea who the contact was at ESL. We though it was Gus earlier, but he said he answered to someone else at ESL. We didn't know for sure until your phone rang. You see, your friend from France had a burner phone on him and he said that was what he used to call ESL. The only number in the burner phone was apparently the number for your burner phone. But we only had the number that he dialed but we didn't have a name, until now.

Josh walked up to Jordan and said, "Why did you do this?" Jordan replied, "it's stupid really, I lost all my money in the stock market crash, I lost everything, my savings, my retirement money, … everything, I needed money and a lot of it, the people from France made me an offer I couldn't say no too." Josh was now face to face with Jordan and he said, "You put my family and friends in danger you S.O.B. Right then, there was a scream of excitement when Ade walked up, Josh turned and hugged Ade. "Thank goodness you are okay! I am so sorry this happened." Ade looked at Jordan who was now in handcuffs. "Is this the guy behind all this?" Josh said, "yes." She slowly walked up to Jordan and said, "Jordan, you put my family in jeopardy and now me again. This is my gift back to you" and Ade proceeded to slap Jordan very hard on his face. Jordan groaned and Ade hugged Josh. Ade turned back facing Jordan again and slapped him one more time. Jordan yelled out, "What was that for?" "That's for being such a jerk at garage sales." The Agents snickered about what just happened, shaking their heads. Dr. Hudson said, "Let's go." and they escorted Jordan to the lobby and out of the building.

21

The next day at work was once again eerie. Josh, Annie, and Jace just looked at each other and said, "What now." Dr. Rico came in and said, "I have a new project for you guys. The military would like us to explore ways we can improve their ability to detect potential defects in their electronic devices. What do you think?"

Josh said, sounds great, Annie, Jace, are you up for the challenge? "You bet jefe," said Jace. "Always an honor to work with you Dr. B!" said Annie. "Dr. Rico, our team is ready to assist," said Josh. Dr. Rico gave two thumbs up.

Josh said, "Hey, you guys have been talking about how great the 'Bats' are. Let's go have a beer and some 'Bats', I'm buying. Dr. Rico, are you going to join us?" Por supuesto señor, gracias [Of course sir, thanks] and off they went to The Venue and to find another adventure awaiting the team.

CPSIA information can be obtained
at www.ICGtesting.com
Printed in the USA
BVHW041939060822
643979BV00001B/18

9 781663 242198